AN IMPRINT OF WHAT BOOKS PRESS | LOS ANGELES

HIPSTER HEAVEN & THE AVANT-GARDE

ALSO BY A. W. DEANNUNTIS

HIPSTER HEAVEN & THE AVANT-GARDE

A NOVEL

A.W. DeAnnuntis

Library of Congress Cataloging-in-Publication Data

Names: DeAnnuntis, A. W. (Anthony W.) author
Title: Hipster heaven & the Avant Garde : a novel / A.W. DeAnnuntis.
Other titles: Hipster heaven and the Avant Garde
Description: Topanga, CA : Giant Claw, 2025. | Summary: "The novel is a
    humorous musical farce and Pythonesque romp among the most famous
    composers of modern western classical music confronting the difficulties
    of converting musical notes into bank notes, recast as leading bar bands
    and performing on instruments which have no counterparts in our current
    musical world while composing and performing for well-known commercial
    producers of films and cartoons"-- Provided by publisher.
Identifiers: LCCN 2025033008 | ISBN 9798998905544 paperback
Subjects: LCGFT: Humorous fiction | Novels | Fiction
Classification: LCC PS3604.E17 H57 2025
LC record available at https://lccn.loc.gov/2025033008

Cover art: Gronk, *untitled*, 2024
Book design by ash good, www.ashgood.com

Giant Claw
363 South Topanga Canyon Boulevard
Topanga, CA 90290

GIANTCLAWPRESS.COM

For Ralph,

and in grateful memory of Jake, and of Slim

TO THE READER–

The following is a work of fiction. Names, characters, places, titles and incidents are all products of the author's imagination or are used only fictitiously. Resemblance to historical events, titles or persons, living or dead, is entirely coincidental.

*Poets and painters alike have always had
the right to take liberties of any kind*

—Horace

*Music is in essence incapable of expressing whatever
you will: a feeling, an attitude, a psychological state,
a phenomenon of nature.*

—Igor Stravinsky

*No poem is intended for the reader, no picture for the
beholder, no symphony for the listener.*

—Walter Benjamin

The modern-day composer refuses to die.

—Edgar Varèse

*Listen, I'm a professional and I just wanna know two
things; where's the beer and when do I get paid.*

—Jimmy Carl Black, the Indian of the group

HIPSTER HEAVEN &
THE AVANT-GARDE

MEANWHILE, CHARLES IVES is attempting once again to play "Crystal Rowed the Boat Ashore" on his C-melody harmocarina and struggles to figure out why it sounds so weird. This remains understandable since until recently he has been dead. Besides, there are twenty-four key signatures available to composers of modern western classical music and Ives has slept with every one of them (his seminal text, "Sleeping With Key Signatures", has never gone out of print), so his difficulty does not involve a particular key signature. The fact is that the tune is written in the Phrygian mode, one that conjures intensity and darkness, just what Ives looks forward to, and yet the tune's chord sequence leaves him baffled and depressed. Still, since he is so often baffled and depressed, he assumes he will fail to recognize himself otherwise.

He has just returned from his latest job at the Snooze & Loose musical café, where he attempts to lead his band, Charlie and the Stink Merchants, to perform his newest orchestral suite, "Every Wall Has A Door", and to premier its hit song, "Amy, You Ain't Maimi", but once again, half the band is drunk and the other half fails to remember the arrangements. For this and other reasons, he now assumes they will be fired at sunrise. But none of that involves key signatures; instead, it's those variously mangy modes which remain an infuriating bafflement.

To Ives's ear those modes resemble hairy and vague shapes obscured in a violet twilight, smoky, corrosive and disturbing. He discovers all this in grade school when his parents force him to take piccolotuba lessons; an instrument he still finds annoying with its tinny, brassy sneering sound, like someone weeping with a mouth full of marshmallows. But as poorly as he understands these modes, he tries to teach his band arrangements that use them in the hope of becoming comfortable with them. As well, that seductive sound, ethereal and yet earthy and even defiantly atonal, should draw a crowd and so make it more likely the band will get paid. But right now his band isn't even close to that.

And if only that was the worst.

Ives recalls his recent visit to the Club You Again? to catch Alban Berg's newest band, Penelope and the Butt-Grabbers (there is, in fact, no Penelope involved with the band, but the name gives it a bit more class), and where, to his dismay, the band blows through thirty-two choruses of its hit sonata, "This Ain't Over", until the audience is reduced to a coma, wheezing and breathless with hysterical exhaustion and several require hospital attention (their previous hit, "The Strange Tale of Cripple Dick", climbs to number seven in the charts and with a bullet). Leaving the club with his ears stunned, Ives shakes his head, annoyed as he so often is of late that he never studied plumbing.

Ives puts pen to paper determined to complete a new ballet/opera he entitles, "Who Are You Performing For?", a melodrama in seven acts about a boy-actor and a girl-actor who fall in love and decide to marry, but their director refuses to allow it, insisting that their marriage will simply annoy everyone except themselves. Only three of the seven acts are written while bits of the others float about in his head in a disharmonious cacophony. Still, his major problem remains: where to place the drum solos. A tornado of flams and paradiddles and rolls and kicks, he doesn't want a solo played too early for fear of chasing his audience away with the threat of an unconscionable blizzard of annoying backbeats. On the other hand, for those few who actually look forward to such a thing, he doesn't want to discourage them from remaining for the entire performance. He plans at least four and spread across the seven movements, but can't decide whether during the happy movements or sad ones. One thing he is certain of; no one taught this in music school. Or at least not in those classes he stayed awake for.

But about Charles Ives's other problems.

Following annoyingly inept performances and despite too many exhausting rehearsals he must admit that his music remains as mysterious to himself as to others, and that admits a lot. With nauseating frequency, what Ives hears inside his head exceeds his grasp so that, more often than not, his music never arrives where he expects it to reach. Even as he begins a new composition, he remains curious to see if he and his composition arrive at the same place at the same time.

And then but suddenly a question comes to his mind, terrifying in its simplicity; does my music sound to others the way it sounds to me?

The question leaves him resigned to the recognition he will require extensive and continuous self-medication. Fortunately, Ives is well-supplied for such an emergency, plus he still has several generous even though unhappy friends. Not as many as in the past and none any longer glad to hear from him but that, after all, is what friends are for. That and also to borrow money from. But he knows how to play the harmocarina very well even if he has never learned to play it in all those dispiriting modes. Each unanswered question leaves him annoyed with despair.

Only weeks before, he discovers that "Crystal Rowed the Pontoon to Shore", another in that anthology of late Renaissance harmocarina sonatas composed by an anonymous Danish monk, is written in the Dorian mode, one more of his least favorite modes, except for all the others, and just as likely to split his lip and cloud his mind. He tries to recall its lyrics, unless the ones that come to mind are to a different song; while unlikely, that suspicion must not be ignored.

Disturbing musical questions give Ives a headache which is why he ignores most such issues even when his friends refuse to allow that. They are his friends, after all, certain they are obliged to torment him with distracting advice pretending to resolve musical and/or sexual cul-de-sacs.

But about "Crystal Rowed the Liter Ashore."

Recently awarded a DUI by a major academic musical institution, Ives berates himself that he must remain ready for the Big Time regardless of how unlikely that time's arrival seems. Curious about its arrival, he remains optimistic someone will alert him when it does even if uncertain who that might be.

Meanwhile, Arthur Honegger completes his most recent railroad locomotive concerto: "Southern Pacific 4-10-2".

Suddenly Bertold Brecht appears. And where Brecht appears, can Kurt Weil be far behind?

––––––––––

Prosperous owner of a chain of dry-cleaners, Brecht has enough money to buy any seat he prefers at this so-called business of composing modern western classical music. He reminds Ives that he will never play "Crystal Rowed the Life-Raft Ashore" correctly regardless of enticing key changes.

Ives refuses to admit his own difficulty memorizing anything longer than a phrase along with the difficulty of performing compositions written in the Lydian mode. To Ives' profound irritation Brecht insists that knowing even a few key changes, Ives should recognize the rest. Such song-guessing is a skill Brecht acquires in his early years as a d. j. on the local radio station.

Seated across from Ives, the more Brecht drinks the louder he gets; this is so typical of composers of modern western classical music that it requires no further comment.

Not being an arrogant man, Ives is confident his skill at song-guessing is at least that of Brecht, although he knows with his formal training he should be better. Until recently, song-guessing remained a key element of every musical training curriculum. Ives acquires his skill studying at a university whereas Brecht is self-taught and annoyingly proud to the point of arrogance. The fact is, Brecht's vanity about his autodidacticism eventually ruins every friendship he pretends to cultivate, which is understandable and perhaps even inevitable, but still, as the owner of a chain of dry-cleaners, not useful. After all, the autodidact always demands to be recognized and acknowledged as the smartest person in the room. Otherwise, what could possibly be the point of being an autodidact?

But Ives has an advanced degree in music, after all, so why should he care what anybody thinks? Self-taught song-guessers annoy him with all their imaginative failures along with their unconcealed contempt for classically trained song-guessers unless they are shapely and female.

Difficulty learning to play any of the variations of that ancient yet infuriating medieval song-cycle still leaves Ives anguished. He recognizes a conflict but not its resolution. If every conflict must have a resolution, Ives is tempted to quiz Brecht on the possibility he might learn something useful. After all, every answer assumes its own question if one simply opens one's ears and looks. Or at least must suggest something that resembles something. This is the nature of that which exists; reality being the ultimate test of whatever may not exist even if assumed otherwise.

Could his world, the world of modern western classical music, be any other way, Ives wonders, because even if all of this is inevitable, he is uncertain he will recognize it as such.

So when Brecht appears on the scene, Ives knows to be wary. People working as dry-cleaners must never be trusted; certain poisonous fumes cause all the wires upstairs to get crossed, or so we must assume and therefore fear. Not necessarily a debility sufficient to put someone in jail, let alone one that would get a composer of modern western classical music killed, a thought Ives refuses to entertain, yet still a trouble serious enough to compel him to borrow money even without hope of repayment.

Not that Ives is ever shy about borrowing money. If anything, he enjoys it since it always assures him at least one person out there who may hate Ives and knows himself poorer because of him, still must worry about his continued good health. Besides, what can any life be worth if no one hates you? Unremarkably, Brecht dissents.

The single fact remains; his failures to perform "Crystal Rowed the Tugboat Ashore" correctly (a variant composed in that ludicrous Mixolydian mode, a vicious bear of a mode with claws like razors yet so much like every other version of its antiquated annoyance) even on the harmocarina. Ives, in his inept performances, draws the ire of those religious musicians who still owe money to J. S. Bach along with those others devoted to the Cult of the Former Virgins, all convinced to follow some delusional Back-To-Bach movement; it must be true that people fail to learn anything until hit over the head and drip blood, and that perhaps more than once.

Deeply dispirited, Ives goes to the Club That's Enough to check out Poulenc's newest band, Frank and The Collected Afflictions, where he's been told Poulenc plans to premier his newest composition, "Containerized Weirdness" for intrabassoon, trombonophone, harmocarina and piccolotuba. Hearing music he could never write and his own band could never play thoroughly depresses Ives, which is why he is here. He is getting very drunk when one of the drummers of Milhaud's last ensemble (not the current one) takes a stool beside him at the bar and starts to tell him a story. According to this drummer (and Ives can no longer remember his name) weeks back he gets talking with a piccolotuba player from Rachmaninoff's last band who is just back from someplace like Germany where they play at some sort of music festival where there are like nine bands on the program and this piccolotuba player says he is really impressed by how many people show up. Drunk and depressed, Ives gives the guy a hard time, insisting Rachmaninoff is a talentless idiot, and besides, something like that could never happen because nobody in their right mind would buy a ticket to a show where he has to wait and listen to eight other bands just so he can hear the one he likes most. The drummer just shakes his head and gives the increasingly drunk Ives a villainous look saying he's just telling Ives what he's heard and that Ives can go fuck himself if he can't even be goddam civil and buy him a beer, and then the drummer walks away. Ives shakes his seriously drunken head recognizing that people don't really like music; what they really like are songs; little snatches of music beneath a stream of words which they can sentimentalize over and then sing in the shower or at a karaoke bar.

Ives's hangover the next morning is so massive he fails to remember he has this conversation, much to his future regret.

All of this, of course, has nothing to do with Igor Stravinsky and his notoriously monstrous hands.

———

A descendent of Modest Mussorgsky who possessed even more enormous hands, Stravinsky thinks nothing of the elephants he causes to be killed. But then again and after all, none of them is paying him money.

Right now, nothing of all that means anything special to Charles Ives, except for that one time when he runs into Stravinsky in the park and without prelude or preamble Stravinsky punches Ives squarely in the nose with one of his very big, very powerful hands. That incident and its injury force Stravinsky to suspend his notorious performance finales of smashing his pianos to pieces in front of his ocean of screaming fans; their disappointment will cost him and his manager. All of this infuriates Stravinsky even if it fails to discourage him from fracturing pianos or punching Ives in the nose.

But we digress and undoubtedly you notice.

In the most recent of those dizzyingly varied and confusing music competitions for which Brecht insists he sit as judge, he assigns Ives' performance several extra points since he feels sorry for the old man. As Brecht hates Stravinsky, this is something Ives especially enjoys. The resulting emotional turmoil bothers Ives's stomach with a particular type of distress he attempts to suppress as it blurs his vision. The scene spread before him would bother even Paul Hindemith.

At nearly the same moment and in a flurry of hysterical energy, Arthur Honegger applies the finishing touch to his newest railroad locomotive concerto entitled, "Mastodon 4-8-0".

Until the appearance of Paul Hindemith and completion of his most recent cantata involving a gruppetto of astonishing complexity and entitled, "Nothing Adds Up", mountain-climbing fails to appeal to modern western music composers even while some insist it once inspired Vivaldi, and for others that it still can, while Hindemith himself even claims it must. Only after climbing treacherous mountains can any composer determined to compose modern western classical music recognize the mystical function of a C minor cord. Finding yourself uncertain, just ask Bartok, but be sure to do so early in the day while he is still sober.

Brecht never climbs a mountain unless he absolutely has to. More relevant, Ives knows that Brecht dismisses Ives' compositions as just so much fluffy hamburger (bland tasting and easily digested). As tempted as he must be, Ives refuses to be pissed-off. Brecht regularly leaves him pissed-off, and yet Ives resists because he must. None of anything will go well and some likely will go very badly otherwise. Unlike many lessons in music, this lesson Ives learns in primary school although he only remembers it occasionally and when it is much too late.

Simply for his own amusement, Hindemith gathers a tidy collection of antique A minor 9th chords and makes a polished wooden box to fit them for display above his fake fireplace with its fake fire in order to torment greedy and unscrupulous but envious orchestrators. Then Ives confesses his fury with Stravinsky and all of those elephants he causes to be killed. Hindemith debates with himself if there is anything there for him, and then at how angry he should be; what is more precious, a piano or an elephant!

All this and yet there remains Ives and his burden of blinding confusion.

Meanwhile, by using a specially-developed microscope, Erik Satie begins to examine every note in the alphabet of music, sorting those most vulnerable to decay and therefore needing to be refrigerated or at least vacuum sealed, as opposed to those least likely to smell bad over a period of time. Acquired at startling expense, Satie's musical microscope allows him to ignore distinctions separating harmocarina playing from all the other playing. The device offers him the ability to scrutinize each note and so anticipate where musical trouble may begin. After all, it is

Stravinsky's note selection as much as his playing which cost so many elephants their lives. Even musicians who are not composers of modern western classical music find this disturbing.

Although it is merely one more cheap, attention-grabbing gimmick like wearing his hair long, it is with Stravinsky's powerful hands that at the end of every performance he destroys his piano, tossing its broken parts to hysterical members of his audience who are pulling off their clothes desperate to be struck by a piece of that piano in such a way it leaves a mark or, even better, draws blood. Thus, elephants find themselves killed dead and their ivory used to make more keys for more pianos which are then destroyed by far-less talented modern western classical music composers trying to be mistaken for Stravinsky and gain undeserved attention.

An unconscionable waste of elephant lives which Stravinsky's theatrics demand, it will be nice for the elephants when he grows tired of busting-up his pianos. Or at least from doing it every single performance!

And you notice that once again we digress.

Stravinsky with his piano-busting is a subject Brecht might discuss with Ives but Brecht knows very little about pianos or Stravinsky or anything that might inform Ives since it has nothing to do with dry-cleaning.

And to the bafflement of railroad locomotive symphony enthusiasts everywhere, Arthur Honegger completes his latest railroad locomotive symphony entitled, "Olomana 0-4-2".

————

Hindemith is pals with Ives in high-school as that kid no one will sit next to since he bathed so rarely. Knowing all of this, Ives also knows that eventually he will inherit an insurance company where his work will be to sit at a desk and play with paperclips and secretaries. So why should he care about what other people think about how he smells, or plays the harmocarina for that matter? This also suggests an excuse for failing to learn the notes to "Crystal Rowed the Canoe to Shore", composed in that baffling Locrian mode, one more musical mode resembling every other, where everything written backward makes sense.

But high school is like that for most of us; time spent struggling to become comfortable among cannibals.

Hindemith conjures a new project he needs Brecht to help pay for since once again Hindemith has so little money that he needs to pay someone to tell him how little he has. But then again, he is certain Brecht will do anything for a break from his wife and kids. Hindemith does not need Brecht to do much, but he hopes Brecht will agree at least to that.

When he hears it explained, Brecht realizes he is deeply annoyed by Hindemith's limitless needs even while he pretends to give the question serious thought. Having failed to kill Albert Roussel in an embarrassing reversal, Brecht can only envy Schoenberg's success at such assignments and wonders if his own career murdering composers of modern western music will ever take off. Practice in every profession must begin slowly but he really needs the money. Composers of his ilk earn nothing regardless of how famous they become, demonstrating once again that being famous does not instantly fill pockets. Opportunities are rare, and so people with other people in mind who they want murdered by persons other than themselves are precious.

Once again Ives brings out his harmocarina, slaps it against the palm of his hand and launches into "Crystal Rowed the Ocean Liner Ashore"; written in the Aeolian mode. He attempts to play it in D major, the only key in which he is comfortable but fails, for which he grits his teeth.

––––––––

As mentioned, there have been many musical keys in Ives' life, but a fling is never a relationship or even a romance, unless it is a relationship disguised within time and space and not costing much money. A key signature, after all, is more a permission than a commitment, especially as the commitments of the composer of modern western classical music are sacred as long as they do not cost much money or otherwise annoy or prove inconvenient.

Still, Charles Ives is creative. He understands that in his next musical comeback, whether accompanied by Brecht or Hindemith, he will need a particularly great plan or more heavy artillery. So eventually he calls Stravinsky and when Stravinsky hears what he is being asked, he becomes annoyed. Whether Ives kills Hindemith or Hindemith kills Ives, Stravinsky sees that soon there will be room at the top for the likes of him. He is finally relieved to complete his most recent composition for an intramelophone quintet he titles, "Your Future As A Vampire" and to absolutely no one's notice. With both composers gone, there can only be even more room for him as himself. Besides, they each have that creepy romantic smell surrounding them like the aroma of unwashed socks which turns Stravinsky's stomach.

And then one evening while Stravinsky is snuggling with one of his mistresses whose name he cannot at the moment remember (one of the tall, blond ones), and she tells him that on her last trip she attended a sort of music festival where several bands (she doesn't remember how many but insists there were too many) performed over several days on the same stage and she was surprised that so many people showed up. But at this moment Stravinsky is so ensnared by non-musical thoughts he misses pretty much everything she tells him, and after falling asleep recalls nothing except that he really likes having mistresses as long as they are not too expensive.

———————

Ives completes his most recent grant application, this one sponsored by the Society for the Promotion of One-Armed Paperhangers and titled the Parking Space Award for reasons no one can be bothered to guess but by which Ives knows he will be rejected. Oddly, on this occasion Ives does not need the money, but by demanding to be considered for this award he is determined to remind his contemporaries that even when occasionally dead, he must not be taken for granted or otherwise cheated of his small amount of hard-earned money. Since his contemporaries must know how much money he doesn't have, his application will piss off many of those who are certain they deserve the money more. But things must be changing since nothing comes to rest for very long or at the same location or according to a particular wish.

Subsequent to his most recent demise, Darius Milhaud assures friends that his assassin approaches and when that person emerges, they should assume that person has been sent by Schoenberg. And yet, things never work out that way and for obvious reasons (Milhaud's most recent composition, "The One Who Never Mattered" a quartet for intramelophone, triggers torrents of unpleasant criticism; his subsequent composition, written in response to that hostility, is entitled, "None Of This Will Matter Either"). When both are ignored he decides this can only be the prelude to his next composition, "None Of This Will Be Recorded", each of these is composed with many clusters of off-beat phrase constructions, which makes Milhaud smile.

Meanwhile, members of Stravinsky's newest band, Igor and the Skull-Crushers, are certain he has decided to fire them and then set off on some self-aggrandizing solo tour, confident he will make more money since he will have no one else to pay, and they are not happy.

Despite a fog of bitter jealousy that enwraps Stravinsky's band in a corrosive rancor, a symphony emerges from the pen of Milhaud that resembles a work Stravinsky has already written. Stravinsky becomes irate; in the role of a profoundly irate Russian composer, Stravinsky has no equal. In fact, if his friends do not restrain him he will dig up Mozart's grave just so to punch him squarely in his dead but also very old-fashioned classical music composer's nose. All are certain Stravinsky is intolerably vindictive.

As none of this is news to Ives, he refuses to be curious. The end of the twentieth century approaches and conflicts intensify and mortality explodes among composers with dispiriting frequency to approach epidemic proportions. Few will forget the Philip Glass/Steve Reich championship bout; if Reich fails to land that sucker-punch in the third round which the ref pretends not to see, modern western classical music will be less modern although perhaps more musical. As unlikely as it seems, even Ives sees this, although only after Glass takes Reich to court in a misguided attempt to get his crown back.

Bertold Brecht insists as the owner of a dry-cleaner's he will not soil his hands with neurotic disputes among hair-brained and half-trained composers. But once again he needs to gather a new band before assassinating any more rivals. And as everyone agrees, snipers never come cheap if they're any good.

Plus also, as Franz Schubert always says, there's no drug like money.

If Stravinsky knows just one thing, it is that Milhaud better stop bothering him with late-night phone calls, sobbing and drunk, about whatever happened to those good old days when audiences still threw underwear at them. Stravinsky is relieved that whatever comes from that pile of musical compost Milhaud will leave behind to the misery of his three wives and eight kids to divvy-up—and good luck to the lot of them—at least he will never need to listen to that maudlin moaning again. Obvious and transparent about how relieved he feels with this well-earned demise, Stravinsky will be spared Milhaud's illiterate ramblings conjured with ears closed and his hand open palm-up. So with Milhaud dead again, he wonders if he is expected to write some hypocritical obit for him to appear in Rolling Stone. Not that Stravinsky ever reads Rolling Stone, although he still likes to look at the pictures.

And like so many others, Stravinsky finds himself more baffled than annoyed when Arthur Honegger completes his most recent railroad locomotive symphony entitled, "Santa Fe 2-10-2".

––––––––

Ives knows he must make a decision and he doesn't want to. His old roommate from college, Wallace Stevens, calls him eager to commiserate over the most recent passing of Milhaud, but Ives is the wrong composer of modern western classical music for that exercise, having so often suggested Milhaud wrap himself in a trombonophone quartet and never wake up.

Ives has nearly finished his newest double-sonata for harmocarina accompanied by an intrabasoon quartet and based on the traditional folk-melody, "You Better Take It With You", fortunately composed in the Ionia mode, the only mode that seems to Ives to resemble music that someone might recognize as such and perhaps even pay money for. What bothers him, as with so many past projects, is the drum solo; where to place it in the score, how long it should last, and should the score include a second drum solo, perhaps just before the conclusion. Drum solos remain annoying and uninteresting even though preteen crowds appear to enjoy them. Other drummers are so vehemently critical that they complain when they discover that a particular drum solo sucks (one of the colorful albeit technical terms by which drummers communicate contempt for the failure of fellow-practitioners, unlike, say, a violinist who simply becomes depressed). But none of that is guaranteed and drum solos continue to decorate while failing to entertain or otherwise offer any meaningful contribution.

Stravinsky remans impossible to intimidate, especially after his most recent and oddly-rewarding composition for glass trombone and piccolotuba quartet entitled, "So Much Can Never Be Said", in which he avoids everything involving drums or drummers or any other percussive instrument. This embarrasses his friends as well as at least one of his ex-wives (either the second or the third, the only one who still answers his phone calls), a former beauty-queen, fashion model and heiress to several well-known and lucrative boondoggles and still in the market for more.

Conflicting emotions relieve any pressure from Brecht to dig out his modern western classical music composer's shot-gun. Unlike Schoenberg, he is not eager to shoot any particular music composer, but rather, each of those talentless critics who disparage accomplished works from serious composers without any attempt at a coherent justification, but instead issue their so-called critiques as obscure harangues in gutturally-pitched voices and using terminology no one understands. Written language, after all, can say nothing true or accurate or even interesting about music.

So Ives wonders how any non-musician might genuinely enjoy the occasional shooting of some stray composer of modern western classical music in exchange for a large amount of cash money and without a tremor of regret. Certain composers are tempted to give such behavior a pass. Despite his chain of dry-cleaners, Brecht is eager to be recognized a composer of modern western classical music. Yet few who are familiar with the dry-cleaning industry are in the dark about the cut-throat competition which might dampen enthusiastic spirits elsewhere.

But considering the popularity of certain stage-act gimmicks like Stravinsky's breaking-up of his pianos, there must be something comparable for Ives to cultivate and which also will add to his income. He wonders if he should allow his hair to grow and dye it some distracting color, as his college roommate and otherwise unfamous Wallace Stevens so often insists others soon will.

––––––––––

In a codex added to Scriabin's last will and testament, he insists the parking lot across the street from his home be handed over to Brecht in gratitude for his service to the musical community by dry-cleaning the clothes of performing musicians. Happily, no one asks whether this service to the broader musical community helps anyone except Brecht.

But others see peculiar things coming; Stravinsky challenges Scriabin's will in court, since the property Scriabin offers to Brecht is the same that Stravinsky wants for his new piano warehouse. Even in death—and Scriabin's this time appears permanent—he remains more viscous than most composers of modern western classical music can tolerate. But Stravinsky refuses to endure any of this lying down or remaining dead.

The tiny bit of help that Brecht offers Ives gives him too much to think about. Ives wonders whether to continue to compose modern western classical music (he is about to complete an octet for perhaps eight instruments, but not very loud ones, which he finally entitles, "The Case For Foot Enlargement"). Baffled, Ives admits that so few offers are being made for music involving foot-enlargement that he considers a return to insurance instead. Yet he still enjoys the glamour of modern western classical music composition with all the bright lights and noisy adulation but most of all the young girls—all the young girls.

Baseball may be an artform, but western classical music, especially modern western classical music, is still where the most profound fun resides; just ask Stravinsky.

Arthur Honegger then accidently completes his most urgent and potentially lucrative railroad locomotive symphony: "Norfolk & Western 2-6-6-4".

Following an infuriating conversation with Shostakovich, Stravinsky wonders where all of the best movie contracts are going. Is that younger generation sculking in the wings eager, even desperate, for Stravinsky and his generation to kick off and very permanently so that they can get some of this limited but lucrative work for themselves? In a cloud of guilty nostalgia, Stravinsky recalls a conversation with Maurice Ravel where eventually he laughs that Ravel is nothing more than old and pathetic. Unless that embarrassing memory actually stars Claude Debussy? It cannot involve Scriabin who is likely already as dead as he ever will be and remains intolerant of persuasion.

Concerning Paul Hindemith; although his music nauseates Ives, he likes Hindemith as a person even when Hindemith drinks too much and then commandeers Ives' couch to snore even more loudly than when he sleeps anywhere else. Annoyed, Ives mentions this to Hindemith who simply denies he has ever snored and so he will drink however much he wants. Ives sees a quandary wherein resignation resembles victory since it contains no defeat.

Drinking, like composing modern western classical music, resists comment even when it involves composer/musicians who snore like bulldozers in reverse. Considering a composer of the stature of Hindemith, Schoenberg hesitates before concluding it is time for him to speed up his plan for musical assassination if he ever expects his own music to gather appropriate attention.

Much is said about alcohol and its consumption, but Ives is determined to consider issues other and elsewhere while he drinks. And anything said about Hindemith's drinking can likely be said about most other composers. Ives is an empirical and well-practiced drinker and nothing like his college roommate Wallace Stevens who, he recalls with a grimace, drinks even more than a fish which justifies his flights to Florida despite his hatred of mosquitos and humid sunshine and the tourists, oh the goddamn tourists. Ives reminds himself that Stevens pretends to be some kind of picture painter, so what else should he expect?

What most intrigues Ives about his own music is that it sounds so modern and yet so oddly antiquated, groaning open to offer itself to the salivating jaws of a grey and sharp-edged future as if it was the past. Stravinsky's music, on the other hand, sounds so viciously modern it rattles like a clanking motor while still sounding newer than yesterday. It all so reminds Ives of Shostakovich, even if Shostakovich's recent work amounts to writing brief tunes for television advertisements (his compositions for the Karl the Kat cartoons remain better than just journeyman's practice, as if preparing the listener for something nearly interesting). After the fist-fight between Shostakovich and Prokofiev in the parking lot of the Chalk & Cheese Lounge, Ives becomes optimistic. Happily, Pablo Picasso steps in to break up the fight even at the cost of a split lip and broken right index finger. To the relief of most, Picasso is just one more tone-deaf poet certain that writing modern western classical music is a snap, and so does it on the side as if certain he knows what he is doing and that the approval of others is inevitable even when half-hearted. But even to non-musicians it is obvious that if he knows anything about modern western classical music, he doesn't know much and has forgotten the rest.

———

Ives is reminded that if he hopes to get one of those annoying and time-consuming Nobel Prizes in music he needs to avoid fist-fights with other composers. Completion of its application paper-work demands an entire day and that is just for the first round and well before he is allowed to submit anything resembling a musical composition. But being paid to compose modern western classical music remains impossible without one of those ludicrous awards unless one is ready, like Prokofiev, to crank out hours of brain-deadening ambience music (as if anyone even knows what that is). But as with every other conjecture, making a living as opposed to earning serious money are so utterly different that their distinction resembles a joke without a punchline. Even when Ives finally speaks with Stravinsky without having his nose punched in, the topic is money and its absence.

Ives has one question; with Hindemith again returned to life, what has Stravinsky heard about these so-called music festivals? Ives remains certain the only reliable way to make a living while writing music is to be bound hand-and-foot to a stifling and utterly abusive recording contract tying that composer to a dinky, no-name, no-pockets recording label. After all, sales of those ridiculous t-shirts with vicious language and salacious images remain where the real money is made. Like most composers of modern western classical music, Ives earns as much from the sale of t-shirts as any stacks of recorded discs. After all, t-shirts drive an audience by informing it when a new recording comes into existence while describing to that audience the band's weltanschauung. Ives is regularly assured that such advertising is precious beyond value, no matter how saddening or dispiriting or just stupid that assertion must be.

But Paul Hindemith, even dead, is deeply clever and more clever than Ives enjoys admitting. What Hindemith figures out, and no one else figures out, is that the certain assurance of future musical success before being dead is by becoming popular with the youngest audience one can address. He learns this lesson from Prokofiev's composition, "Tunafish a' La Mode", a five-piece cantata, none of whose parts are sung in English. All of those little kids at Saturday matinees, screaming and throwing-up and hurling their panties onto the stage are in fact stacks of future money stashed in a future bank and assure Prokofiev he will earn money for the next decade during which those same kids will age painfully and thus turn against Prokofiev and his music, certain he is hopelessly smelly and old-fashion and even laugh embarrassed to have enjoyed his recordings. Following all this, they will amuse each other with clever quips displaying their contempt of those who have incompetently aged. But the children of those same fans, relieved that Prokofiev is no longer relevant, will, from the vantage point of their own youth, thumb their collective noses at their rapidly antiquating parents and rediscover "Tunafish a' La Mode" and thereby provide Prokofiev a bit more of that do-re-mi no one who continues to breathe can do without for very long.

Happily for those still curious, Arthur Honegger overcomes self-doubt and a brief but thrilling cocaine addiction to complete his most ambitious railroad locomotive symphony, entitled "Pacific 4-6-2".

In a vein similar but different, Ives discovers that having learned Prokofiev's lesson Arron Copeland is preparing his own ballet/opera hopeful of getting paid by someone for composing something. So much like himself and despite all the music he has composed, Ives fails to conjure that one catchy Christmas recording, or, instead, that peculiarly popular ditty which becomes everyone's summer anthem, or even the soundtrack to a holiday cartoon-comedy-variety-show special extravaganza. Ives, after all, is confident he is a clever-enough guy and certainly as clever as Hindemith. Hindemith, however, early on figures out that the only reliable way to earn money writing music is to teach high school; that, at least, appears praiseworthy even if crippling.

Hindemith secludes himself at a dinky high-school in the middle of the woods impossibly far from the excitement of modern western classical music composition. How he tolerates this brain-deadening isolation leaves Ives choked with rage unless it is boredom; often he mistakes their difference. But Hindemith is paid a regular salary and so manages to support a girlfriend or two. And happily for him and them, he will likely continue to receive that salary from one year to the next. Ives consoles himself that over time certain advantages tend to even out, but only over time, and the amount of time needed never provides reassurance. His best chance is that someone dies and leaves him a nice pile of money; who and when remain tautological mysteries.

Recognizing himself now out of useful options, Ives concludes that he must call Stravinsky. Ives assumes Stravinsky has leverage with the local musician's union shop-steward, Eugene Ormandy. When he first moves here, Ives is assured the only way to get steady work is to make a pal at the union hall, but Ives still hasn't even gotten a union card, and he's assured he'll never get one until he pays his back-dues. And for all of that, he will need even more money which he will then need to borrow. He wonders whether this all amounts to a merry-go-round where a stack of money keeps changing hands, unless something else is making Ives dizzy.

He considers helping Stravinsky find more elephants to kill, after which then he might at least be paid. Not that this appeals to Ives but he needs the money badly and as everyone agrees, only money attracts money while everything else repels it.

But if all of that is true, how is it that Hindemith earns any money at all?

Something remains absent from this account; peculiar but significant blanks beg to be filled in. Ives hates to think of his existence in this way, but how else can anyone imagine his own future or any of those futures which appear available to composers of modern western classical music?

When Schoenberg returns to life, Ives finds himself still adrift in a swamp of primordial nostalgia where from within his memory faces arise of those he has borrowed money from but have not come to mind for a long time. Is there any use to such roiling recollections; are these anything more than discouraging distractions? Is there a benefit from such reflections? If it's merely money he needs, how depressed should he be? Ives worries he is about to answer that question but not a way he will enjoy.

———————

For composers of modern western classical music, the ascent to fame and material success remains steep and stoney. But just consider; as there has already been a great quantity of classical music composed, why compose any more? How much is enough and when will the point of too much be reached? More darkly, is any of this even a question someone like Ives should bother considering? Or is it just one more question front-loaded with negation and self-doubt and whose response he is really going to hate. As Ives thinks about all of this, something Hindemith once said in passing comes to his mind: one can never have too many trobonophones but it is always possible to have too many players. At a different time and for a different reason Ives suspects he nearly understands what that means until that suspicion suddenly dissipates like a mist at sunrise.

Utility is the justification for every other thing but recently threatens to be held up as the only certain measure of reality. Ives recognizes this as a question modern western classical music composers ponder and debate and then eagerly flee until they have become overwhelmed by age. A composer can turn away from this question, but the question never abandons the composer; not if one truly is a composer of truly modern western classical music.

The burden of modern western classical music composers: deep memories conjuring towers of hours miserably spent practicing to play instruments no one cares to hear, all sparkling with black dots signifying nothing beyond themselves.

But the additional challenge? That all past and securely dead classical music composers expect to be remembered and their compositions praised within the shadow of a large stack of money; there is no future without a past piled with packages of disposable income. Just as for Ives, so for Ferruccio Busoni; the past and the future resemble each other even when, despite specific quantities of money involved, they are certainly different. This is one reason Ravel and Satie no longer speak to each other even though on numerous occasions they have been dead French men. Marcel Proust, another frequently dead French man, agrees to pass written notes between their dead selves, each of which will refer to small amounts of money needing to be accumulated and passed on unless ignored.

On the other hand, Satie is paid so much money he is no longer bothers to balance his checkbook; especially since that exercise reminds him of the misery of high school algebra classes. Just as he has no idea how much money he has, he no longer recalls those contracts he has signed. After all, having bet the rat races and so often losing, he has embraced the uncanny skill of always mistaking the losing for the winning rat. As a quirk of baffled empathy, Satie refuses to ignore his moral obligation to bet on losing rats; otherwise losing rats will become depressed and then desperate if no one bets on them. Thus, Satie flaunts his ignorance of those inevitable hurt feelings of some otherwise random particular musicians and the resulting distortions of modern western classical music. Modern western classical music is already hard enough to listen to; an additional emotional burden or psychological complexity will make it unfathomable. Satie recognizes that this burden is not entirely his fault, but he is incapable of reducing its difficulty.

Because there is, after all, Stravinsky.

To the surprise of many, Arthur Honegger wrestles successfully with his lower self, kicks his cocaine addiction permanently and then composes another of his intriguing railroad locomotive symphonies; this one entitled, "Allegheny 2-6-6-6".

Ives learns that those unshaven, unbathed and overfed Russians are determined to turn modern western classical music into a peculiarly flabby and dispiriting exercise in bad taste. Had certain younger composers heeded the advice of Debussy or even Busoni, the progress of modern western classical music would be different. Instead, they follow Dr. Disaster; Arnold Schoenberg.

Schoenberg poisons his first composer just after the war, certain that the young man in question, one of those types so sensitive they must wear glasses, has composed music which will be chosen ahead of Schoenberg's for a film for Republic Pictures entitled, "Sundays With Robbie", a film about a powerful and brilliant robot that adopts a human suburban family, following which terrifying disasters and much hilarity ensues. With this successful musical homicide, Schoenberg is startled to experience a profound sense of gratification at the demise of one more arrogant, illiterate but also foolish upstart. His poisonings of up-coming composers eventually become less accurately targeted and therefore more poetic. And it disturbs him deeply that he finds he enjoys watching youthful and fragile composers of modern western classical music gasp turning purple unto death. Obviously, few would have predicted any of this.

Intriguingly, Korngold suspects his neighbor Schoenberg's behavior almost immediately but as a product of that engrained cowardice of most composers of modern western classical music he tells no one. That distressing decision comes about in part because Korngold's gardener has recently run off with Korngold's favorite cook. Following this discovery, he spends his midnight hours stapling flyers to various telephone poles in his neighborhood begging for information that will lead to her return. And to his withering embarrassment, he is recognized by several of his neighbors while at this and inevitably comments follow. But this is an entirely separate story and so must not distract us further.

As with so much else in the life of a composer of modern western classical music, certain murders transpire as mere flirtations, mildly amusing but thoroughly passing fancies that gesture to piss-off the old folks or piss-off Brahams or piss off any other equally old and smelly composer often aided by a nod and a wink and hows-by-you; good-humored distraction, meaningless in any important way and certainly nothing to wonder about.

Between utilitarian murders Schoenberg cranks out several tunes which get some air-play and to the astonishment of Ives along with certain other composers far less visible than Schoenberg. Indeed, no one with a checkbook embarrasses themselves by beating a path to Ives' door. Still, it does not demand a very active imagination to see just past the horizon and how all things will suddenly but inevitably become different and not in a good or enjoyable way. After that, who knows how quickly this peculiar infection with accompanying psychic inflammation will spread or how debilitating it will prove in the end to be.

And then a drummer Ives has recently met accidently gives him a couple of ideas Ives has never had before. The chords underlying these suggestions seem to fall easily beneath Ives' fingers on his melophonium, so at first he fails to question their quality, satisfied simply with their quantity along with their absence of color. At the same time, this drummer—whose name he can no longer recall, to his profound relief—also introduces Ives to a couple of melophonium players of astonishing and therefore reassuring ineptitude. He remains however humiliated and embarrassed by the continuing situation that he still cannot play "Crystal Rowed the Kayak Ashore", on his harmocarina and then he hears these melophonium players also fail, he merely smiles with nausea and self-doubt, annoyed by his lack of self-confidence as much as by absence of skill of these melophonium players along with their indifference to the high-end music generally.

———————

Despite or regardless of all of this unless it is because of this, Ives recognizes that until he puts together another band able to play his music, or at least someone's music, he will remain on the outside looking in. What, after all, does Stravinsky or Schoenberg or even that idiot Alban Berg with his brain-dead teenage female chorus, have that he does not, except money plus a band that plays the music he writes with at least rough accuracy?

Actually and in fact, a sober, well-rehearsed and enthusiastic band, which otherwise resembles absolutely none Ives has ever been part of, would provide an inspiring change. Perhaps the age of miracles has not passed after all or at least not completely.

And yet in the end, he is unable to forget that above everything else, a band costs lots of money and the larger and more professional, the more money. Also the longer he maintains that band, even if only long enough to learn his music, the more all of that must add to that band's cost. Despite his skill at borrowing money, Ives is unable to imagine how to borrow enough to pay for the rehearsal time needed to learn his music.

In short, Ives wanders within a difficulty corroded with money and with no obvious pathway out.

––––––––––

Recently returned from the dead, Milhaud and Hindemith enjoy one more falling-out, even more serious than their last. Despite having collaborated on several of the decade's most popular film scores, including three annoying, noisy and certainly unnecessary science fiction movies that batter their audience's ears with impossible noises to demonstrate they are necessary in order to make a full orchestra sound like several tractor-trailers colliding, those film scores provide stacks of awards attached to bundles of money. Thus. their dissolution as a music-writing team shocks and dismays their fans but which only becomes worse when those fans take sides. Milhaud's fans insist the break-up has everything to do with Hindemith's greed and overwhelming ego. Hindemith's fans, on the other hand, insist that it is Milhaud's zany Asian girlfriend and her dope-addled jazz-music addicted buddies who insist Milhaud write only music that no one will listen to let alone try to play. All of this, or perhaps only most of it, eventually fractures their collaboration.

Ives drifts between fury and depression. How can these gangsters mess up their splendid meal ticket? Have they forgotten what the rest of us so long ago realized, that the only good musician is a dead musician and so every live music performer represents a regression from an otherwise failed art?

And most especially drummers.

It occurs to Ives that with those two gone from the scene, despite the minimal space they occupied, their departure offers the chance to claw back certain Grammys others have ensnared and hoarded—just penetrate those buggers. With this turmoil other musicians look about, certain their next paycheck is just around the corner. But for anything useful to be accomplished, Ives must borrow money even while by that prospect he is secretly pleased.

Given all that fails to happen, Ives considers resuming his career at professional song-guessing, one he prefers to professional wrestling which paid him serious money yet did him far more harm than good. Still, Ives is certain Bertold Brecht must eventually retire from song-guessing. But the more Ives thinks about this, the more discouraged he becomes. Despite being occasionally dead, Brecht would need to retire permanently and that is unlikely to happen, at least soon. So perhaps Ives should embrace the responsibility and assassinate Brecht to render him at least temporarily dead. But Ives also notices that of late Brecht surrounds himself with muscular and dull-witted bodyguards so that the challenge of his assassination has become difficult and perhaps even dangerous. Besides, he assumes Brecht has stored away a pile of unreleased recordings, and so being dead will not make him less popular. If anything, death could make him wealthier given how popular and profitable dead composers of modern western classical music inevitably become. Except, of course, for Ives.

Although his financial profile does not appear likely to improve, Ives still needs his own band and the money that band will devour (rehearsal hall rental, recording engineer rental, girlfriend rental, payment for practice time, plus so many drugs and in such quantities; none of which are becoming less expensive). To climb that ladder to musical stardom among the composers of modern western classical music, a band is the only rung he needs, but he needs at least that one.

The more Ives ponders all of this, the more discouraged he becomes. Will certain untalented, undisciplined, and uninspired Russians squat motionless atop the musical charts smug and grinning as if they owned the place? At least Satie, no matter how badly he smells or how poorly he speaks French or otherwise appears desperate to be mistaken for a musician, is not a Russian. Same with Debussy and Ravel and even Scriabin, although Ives now wonders if Scriabin really is French; Russians are crazy enough to insist they are in fact French; Ives has learned this all too well. He assumes that in the end he will need to speak to Stravinsky; one more difficulty that will keep him awake at night.

Ives believes that at the end of every thought hovers a question, and he wonders whether Shostakovich or Prokofiev or even Stravinsky has ever been burdened with that notion. So, is this what is costing him sleep? His desire to be known as a major composer of modern western classical music has never demanded improvement of his life. On reflection, Ives is relieved to distinguish his failure to succeed as just that. And yet there remain certain Russians who Ives is certain he should do something about without knowing what that might be.

His most urgent need remains to locate musicians appropriate to his music; that is, broke enough to need the work but not so crappy that no one else would hire them. Each musician must be nearly good enough to be hired in another band. He certainly will never afford to hire any of those rich musicians whose names others already know.

No, his musicians must be those who don't want to be hired; his musicians must do little more than argue and sleep. Sleepy, grumpy musicians; the only sort that might appreciate even if never understand his music. Then again, what does understanding music even amount to? Is understanding music simply to display the ability to compose music exactly like it? In fact, what can it mean to understand anyone's music?

Can Ives claim, let alone demonstrate, that he understands the music of any composer not named Charles Ives? Worse, how might such understanding be demonstrated? Is understanding music like understanding algebra, or more like understanding words in a foreign language? After all, understanding a foreign language assumes the ability to substitute one foreign word for one commonly-known. And understanding algebra seems little more than the ability to reduce a complicated problem into something simple. So how does any of that resemble understanding of music? Ives is not even prepared to guess.

Meanwhile, Honegger, after a vile and lingering illness complete with disgusting bodily functions, finishes his most radical and atonal railroad locomotive symphony yet; he titles it, "Texas 2-10-4".

———————

Shostakovich and Prokofiev with their butts flat on the asphalt in the shade of the pool house with the filter rumbling on and off behind them, are drinking quart-bottles of warm beer beside the tennis court behind Milhaud's house, much to Milhaud's annoyance. Since he is no longer dead he is eager to play a game of tennis despite the fact he is lousy at the game and will lose and test his capacity for additional annoyance. And then Rachmaninoff shows up insisting he wants to play. The two of them are just drunk enough to tell him to fuck-off even though it isn't even their tennis court. Earlier, being slightly more sober, they agree that the winner of their match will sleep with the ravishing Maria Ouspenskya, who consents to this arrangement only on the condition that the winner writes a symphony titled for her. Composers of modern western classical music find it nearly impossible otherwise to get truly hot dates, so this sort of agreement appears eminently fair and satisfactory to all parties even if unnecessarily complicated.

Just before all of this, Erik Satie returns to town fronting his new 16-piece band called Noise Reconsidered, (12 percussionists on various forms of percussion, plus intrabassoon, glass trombone, harmocarina and piccolotuba). As a result of some hysterical confusion, first-night tickets sell-out almost instantly. Ives calls a pal in the stage crew and in exchange for a sonata for unaccompanied autoharp, he gets a back-stage pass. The new band's performance is such a complete success that the audience, hysterical in its collective enthusiasm, throws plastic cigarette lighters onto the stage, one of which unfortunately strikes Satie just above his left eye, causing him to announce from the stage that he will never again perform in this bleeping berg. Hearing this, local law enforcement sighs with relief.

From that performance of Satie's band with its comically goofy tunes with impossible to recall titles and nonsensical lyrics, Ives steals two intriguing ideas.

First is that he must never hire more than three drummers; three drunken drummers are more than enough for any band, especially since sober drummers have yet to be identified, located, trained or even invented. Next, he must never hire more than five glass trombone players since even with that number there will be bickering unless thoroughly drunk; glass trombone players tend to be insufferable and back-stabbing prima-donnas in bitter contempt of reality. All of that can only be bad for any band that pretends to perform modern western classical music as if it might somehow sound like real music. With all this in mind, Ives considers hiring several tone-deaf intrabassoon players, unable to hear each other precisely and therefore unable to disagree successfully. So how many other players will he need playing what other instruments in order for them all eventually to be paid?

With all of this, Ives is chilled by one more soul-sickening but also baffling query; should he continue to write music unlikely ever to be performed? Then he wonders if his most recent music sounds especially hairy and dark as if composed in modes no one has ever heard. This is a surprise but also a disappointing mystery. After all, who can describe what they have never heard. The shape and tenor of Ives' music oscillates unevenly between delirium and belligerence and boredom. For a moment he endures the temptation to ask that Andre Breton, as the most popular of lyricists despite being fired from his job as p. a. announcer at the rat races, to scribble a few shapeless and impenetrable and preferably annoying lyrics to everyone's bafflement and for no one's edification. On reflection he recalls the old musical proverb that drunks should never hire drunks to direct drunks; as a working musician, he has heard this so many times he no longer remembers who first said it even while he remains grateful that someone did. Still, it takes a long time to discover anything true, so once done, he should refuse to forget it no matter the desire otherwise.

Once again and to the surprise of many, Arthur Honegger completes another new railroad locomotive symphony, this one entitled, "Union Pacific Big Boy 4-8-8-4" and he can hardly wait to hear what it sounds like when played by a band of sufficiently even if vaguely professional musicians.

Shostakovich assures Ives that Stravinsky struggles with the temptation to start one of those trick-and-roll bands everyone is talking about where no one in the band or even among the fans knows much about music even while insisting they know what they like. None of the other composers of modern western classical music think well-enough of Stravinsky to discourage this illusion, and some secretly envy him. The least they can do—and for Stravinsky each does as little as possible—is steal his music instead of helping him to form such a band; certainly a disastrous fantasy for one more deliriously wealthy but poorly-regarded composer.

Most of the successful trick-and-roll bands sport piccolotuba sections to discourage song-guessing or kazoo-playing or any other form of audience participation. In this way they hope to confuse audiences into believing that something musical is going on and what they hear is the closest they should expect to get to music. Other instruments are included in order to disguise far darker musical thoughts and it is that darkness which seduces listeners even while it repels them. But is it such a good idea to infuse so much darkness into music performed by anemic, hyperactive, barely-dressed and over-sexed and also over-paid trick-and-roll intramelophone players? Thus, a distinction has been recognized. And if so, will teenagers rush out to purchase even more t-shirts with their various salacious images? The music Ives writes is as baffling as it is annoying but also more dispiriting than anything those other composers of modern western classical music conjure. But is the fact that it is baffling what makes it annoying or is it the other way around? There remain piles of ludicrous but creepy speculations concerning trick-and-roll so-called music which they pretend to compose.

This leads Ives to recall Satie's laboratory of musical examination devices. Ives suspects that if he examines his own music at the microtonal level, he will recognize what it is about it which sounds so unlikely that people hate it and therefore refuse to buy it and so prevent it from making any money. Perhaps there are unperceived shapes and gaps hidden within its texts which render his music indecipherable and thereby indigestible. His music should earn him a decent living even if not make him stupidly rich; he knows far too many composers of otherwise unremarkably lousy music, and yet who are inexplicably millionaires, or at least a lot wealthier than Ives and with more girlfriends. How can any of this not be the case when such music is uniformly awful? Ives considers using Satie's microscope to examine this trick-and-roll stuff inexplicably popular and therefore profitable. The more he considers all of this the more eager he is to recognize what makes his own music so annoying. Such an examination might also reveal whatever it is that, despite his irritated chagrin, makes certain music so appealing that people hand over large amounts of hard cash in exchange.

It appears that certain mythopoetic elements contribute to the popularity or lack of popularity of particular compositions. Ives considers forms of music performance involving characters an audience can recognize as such and engaging in dialogues which can be recognized as such in order to highlight elements which prove most engaging, or least distracting, in particular musical examples. Unremarkably, Stravinsky refuses to allow such a device to examine his music, whereas Schoenberg, when its operation is explained, simply laughs loudly and for a long time. But as other composers recognize, that laugh must finally fall on him, even if he will not admit this until his music is no longer modern and smells worse than it sounds.

Ives remains intrigued by this device, especially its capacity to spread self-doubt among popular but otherwise ignorant composers. He is especially charmed by the damage such a device would sow, including anguish and despair among talentless Russians. Ives is certain they are selfishly using far too many minor chords and might leave none for anyone else to use; Russians are just so self-absorbed. And he also assumes these Russians are using every broken rhythm they can lay their hairy hands on. With this he begins to wonder about German composers, including the ones he never thinks about, especially Richard Strauss. Ives wonders when all is said and done whether there will be enough musical devices left for the rest of them.

Having spent years dropping in and out of various trade schools including those apparently involving music, Strauss startles his colleagues by composing a jingle for a car commercial that leaps to the top of the charts and remains there for a month. Convinced of the tune's insubstantiality, Ives envies rather than admires its success. And then Alban Berg and Albert Roussel publish a fatuous and sniveling biography of Modest Mussorgsky where they insist his hands were never very big in their effort to demonstrate that Russians are incapable of being interesting (they even drag Rimski-Korsakov into this argument, much to the chagrin of Busoni). They then emphasize this by insisting Mussorgsky is the composer of the concerto for piccolotuba entitled, "Beans, Beans, Good For Your Heart". Their justification for this absurdity is that they have a deal with the attorneys determined to establish his estate as the sole recipient of colossal royalty payments accumulated over generations. They also anticipate a similar financial agreement when they prevail in a separate lawsuit over the composition of the quintet for glass trombone entitled, "99 Bottles of Beer On The Wall" (based, as musicologist have eventually agreed, on an eleventh century Teutonic wedding song).

When asked, Ives insists he hates all lawyers, especially any goofy enough to sue a musician. He is also contemptuous of their legal assistants and paralegals and especially their comely and elegant legal secretaries. He is certain he is well-informed about such things legal, particularly regarding the abuse of composers of modern western classical music.

In order to get that awful taste of legalisms from his mouth, Ives decides this world deserves a new composition from his pen, maybe a symphony, but certainly not another ballet/opera, and perhaps even en-titled, "The Square-Root of Bugger All". It concerns him, after all, that his music is regarded as cynical and insincere and, particularly painfully, inauthentic despite his efforts otherwise. He knows so many other com-posers guilty of just such musical embarrassments and who are certainly even more cynical and insincere but especially inauthentic than himself. He is also well-aware of how long those so convicted have endured depri-vation of access to drugs and pianos so that eventually they are compelled to teach something to someone.

Ives trembles with jaw-clenched fury at the levels of chicanery involving musical composition; every such suspicion humiliates him where it doesn't infuriate him. Someday someone will step forward to engage in that eternal battle against so much corruption set against too little time and impoverished by far too few F-minor chords wasted among far too many drummers.

———————

Ives discovers that both Shostakovich and Prokofiev are buying pianos which suggests a piano duel is approaching. Both Ravel and Debussy assume this can only be the product of unrestrained self-indulgence, about the only thing they agree on. Like their contemporaries they happily point out the degeneracy of others and the pretentions they must display. Even Berg, never seen to back down from anyone's intrabassoon quartet, proclaims his certainty that all the sound and fury of these laughable piano battles effectively obscures the far more incisive musical gestures common to intrabassoon quintets. Unfortunately, for most those elements merely amount to baffled embarrassment.

Brecht is elated; not least because, considering his sideline as a dealer of used pianos sold from the back doors of his dry-cleaning establishments, every piano destroyed makes the rest of his pianos that much more valuable. Thus, he discovers a way to never lose. But this prospect so disturbs Ives he considers calling his old college roommate, Wallace Stevens, even if confident he has nothing useful to suggest. As in a roller-coaster, Ives' thoughts leave him with serious motion sickness accompanied by a nausea that rises and falls with an intriguing counter-rhythm.

For a composer of modern western classical music, every note is sacred, and this because, as Satie points out elsewhere, each note possesses its own particular color and texture but also aroma and flavor. This is the reason that blind people are never thin, while deaf people almost always are. As well, those various colors and flavors of musical notes gathered together offer a particular profile as musical phrases appear as shadows in outline and thereby charm regardless of how poorly formed. They encourage the rest of us to imagine that despite our ignorance, we know what we are hearing and therefore what we are saying when we talk about music, particularly about modern western classical music, despite every confusion or contingency. And echoes can be neither included nor ignored.

But a bit of knowledge is always more dangerous, even if more baffling, than no knowledge at all.

And, of course, there remains Stravinsky and his pointless infectiousness.

––––––––––

Ives learns that, like Prokofiev and Shostakovich, Stravinsky is purchasing so many pianos he makes himself nearly broke despite all that money Disney is paying him for his cartoon music, something he regards as his own peculiar, if discomforting, specialty. On the other hand, to this point, each piano Berg sends to Stravinsky is reduced to stinking ashes. So it becomes more than just the quantity, but an issue of quality. Stravinsky demands pianos that are at least in tune with themselves. With such quick destruction of so many pianos, he now plays even clunky instruments as long as they have eighty-eight more or less functioning keys. Despite their expense and the absence of quality, certain piano-like objects are being imported from China and also New Jersey. If only they could satisfy Stravinsky's piano-lust.

Antagonism is a large part of Prokofiev's and Shostakovich's musical mythology and therefore attraction, particularly at live performances where their audience looks forward to at least one on-stage punch-up accompanied by a sever piano-bashing. More subtly, their antagonisms are exposed within the scores of their musical compositions as a result of their razor-like precision. Measured by black dots across white staff paper, conflicts are as obvious as knife wounds. Sustained across a range of expression accompanied by poverty, exploitation and depression, conflict remains typical of Russian composers of modern western classical music.

So it comes down to this; by obligating themselves to that which is new, can they admit how annoying the resulting music remains? Even Schoenberg agrees his music attracts far more flies than females and certainly a nearly invisible amount of money. The cure, therefore, must be far worse than the disease. Considering this, what can modern western classical music have to look forward to? Anton Weber then steps forward and to the regret of everyone else.

Weber makes his money as a high-school music teacher who offers keyboard lessons on the side, to the bottomless humiliation of his family members. They had high hopes that, wild oats sown in music school, he would join the electrician's union and lead a normal life, or at least a recognizable one. The several musical jingles he offers to M-G-M for their Tom & Harry cartoons grow out of exercises for his most inept students which is why they sound contemporary even if in an annoyingly sing-songy way, as subtle as the blocks of wood his students already are or must become and very soon, but certainly inevitably.

As exercises they are brief; after all, even his own patience has a limit. Following much trial and error, Weber discovers he cannot keep these exercises brief enough to bridge the attenuated attention span of his students. Thus, his most recent exercises are written using just twelve notes, even if each feels like it goes on forever. To Weber's frustration his students find even these too challenging and none manage to master any of them. Unfortunately for Weber as a high school teacher, annoyance followed by frustration is not a new experience. His superiors explain that embarrassed discomfort justifies those big bucks he is paid following which they then smirk.

Still, several of those compositions somehow make their way to other musical performers determined to discover whether they really are that difficult to write, let alone play. In his adolescence Weber wondered whether there was something wrong with him after all. Over time, that question acquires its own urgency and without resolution, which itself remains unfortunately common among composers.

Ives still recognizes how tricky that question can be. Brecht among several others will insist he steer clear of it if he knows what's good for him. Events scuffle along without threat of resolution until the impossible occurs; Weber's compositions fall into the greedy but sophisticated hands of Schoenberg. Giving even that devil his due, Schoenberg recognizes within this sliver of composition a work which no one else appreciates, let alone enjoys.

In this way, Ives believes, every ending begins.

Stravinsky starts to hire as many drummers as he can track down, certain that otherwise practioners of that disharmonious skill will soon begin searching for jobs as electricians. Even Albert Roussel, who hardly ever notices anything, instantly deciphers the proverbial inscription on the wall. An artificial shortage of drummers, not yet an actual shortage, awaits its resolution when Schoenberg records his own version of Weber's collection of jingle-music, requiring as it does an army of drummers. With this, only the profoundly deaf are safe from aural assault.

As most of Weber's jingles amount to chords attached to unembarrassed drum roll crescendos, Edgar Varese sues over copywrite infringement, having recorded and released a drum quartet with harmocarina solos entitled, "Infinity Begins Here" which only begins to describe that injury. Weber's jingles with Schoenberg's accompaniment get some air-play and earn a bit of money, all to the surprise of nearly everyone, but especially Weber.

———————

Ives finds all of this is too much for his tautly-stretched sensibilities, musical and otherwise, and decides to speak with his old roommate, Wallace Stevens, who is back again sweating noisily among his favorite marshes and swamps. And then, Ives watches as George Antheil enter the room with his mechanical ballet on his arm. Having met this ballet only once he remains impressed by Antheil's companion even if not in an entirely enjoyable way. Ives suspects that seeing one mechanical ballet, he has seen most of them, and it does not occur to him that this may not be the case. Eventually he concedes that this mechanical ballet offers certain charms which resolve his ambivalence, observation being the only confirmation.

First, this mechanical ballet is brightly colored, almost dazzling, as if stitched together of overlapping rainbows. Those colors appear haphazard and yet harmonious and Ives realizes that from a distance it is unlikely he would recognize it as a mechanical symphony or even a mechanical opera. So being a mechanical ballet adds to its charm. But Antheil admits to

Ives that this is his last mechanical ballet unless and until someone pays him serious money because that is how difficult a mechanical ballet is to compose. In a whisper as if fearful of being overheard by this mechanical ballet, he explains the difficulty of writing a mechanical ballet which another mechanical ballet will still recognize as a mechanical ballet, but even more difficult to write one that a non-mechanical ballet will find easy to dance to. Never having aspired to write anything resembling a mechanical ballet, Ives remains indifferent to every detail and so congratulates Antheil on the companionship of such a good-looking mechanical ballet and one of elegant yet startling design.

With this, Antheil assures Ives that Prokofiev plans to compose his own mechanical ballet and so, if Ives is tempted to write a mechanical ballet of his own he better not fool around; the delights of mechanical ballets are in limited supply so that a crisis must loom just beyond the horizon unless it is over the rainbow.

Ives does his best to resist the inevitable just like the rest of us, twisting and squirming even at its suggestion. He wants a conversation with Antheil but out of earshot of his mechanical ballet; such ballets are exceptionally sensitive when being discussed. Ives, Antheil insists, must strike immediately since to hesitate is to lose. Ives is relieved by the urgency of his concern even if dubious of its accuracy or even utility since nearly everyone, at least once in their lives, experiences that dizzying temptation to compose a mechanical ballet.

Ives manages to avoid certain question which he recognizes as merely rhetorical, but such rhetoric does not make a question less a question or less urgent. So perhaps this is one Ives should avoid even attempting to answer.

Then there is Stravinsky, still writing opera/ballets on the toilet before breakfast which, Ives decides, accounts for their peculiar odor. He composes so many opera/ballets he must publish some under pseudonyms which eventually become heteronyms without descending to homonyms, all to the relief of the rest of us or at least most of us.

At this moment Prokofiev decides it is time to write another opera/ballet but this one must not be mechanical. Brecht cannot resist mocking such nonsense, insisting that before Prokofiev begins, he will first need to learn to dance and also count to twelve. Modern western classical music involving dance demands an acceptance of impossible challenges and then the disposition of them quickly regardless of how badly.

When reminded that Stravinsky writes dozens of opera/ballets of his own and never learns to dance or even count to ten, Ives asserts that Stravinsky must have a dancing ghost-writer who provides the basic cadences along with ingenious twists and turns sufficient to startle an audience without upsetting it. Besides, who has ever heard of a composer of modern western classical music who could dance; a bafflement bound to a conundrum.

Ives knows he is right but he also knows he must do something even if that something turns out to be wrong. And then Milhaud, just before he dies once again, composes a series of parodies of Auric's jingles which also resemble jingles which Ives plans to compose just as soon as he finds a matching set of used appoggiaturas. Upon learning that Roussel has miniaturized Stravinsky's jingle and then sold reproductions to Japanese clients who expect to reap profits despite their ignorance of modern western classical music, Ives grinds his teeth.

Days of musical chicanery pass while opportunities for blistering retorts appear to expand rather than evaporate. Each new composition, the moment it appears, is converted into a twelve-note jingle, repackaged and sold to some vastly conglomerated corporation calculating to enhance the perverted employments every organization harbors but which they themselves can neither create nor recognize let alone admire. How can anyone not be embarrassed to facilitate such corruption? The composer of modern western classical music needs higher aspirations even if his pockets are empty; that is the way Ives sees this world and always has but then begins to wonder.

And then Claude Debussy imagines something.

Most composers of modern western classical music pay no attention since Debussy's ideas are never original. Even on those occasions when an idea of his manages to distract certain people's attention, it is unlikely to appear very interesting to very many or for very long. But his neighbors admire Debussy, or at least tolerate his music, or at least do not dislike him or it. Few, it must be admitted, assume he would prove a trustworthy babysitter, thus one less avenue to supplement his meager income. Actually, being a push-over for small children, Debussy enjoys the opportunity to compose brief ditties to amuse them, even if those tunes are regularly stolen by Roussel who then passes them on to Disney where they are published under the pseudonym Caldwell Biscotti and to surprising success. Every organization that oversees the activities of composers of modern western classical music will then be dragged into one more lawsuit, and to the inevitable misery of those thereby afflicted.

To his credit, Brecht remains on the periphery of all this musical bloodshed and looking in. Given the poor decision-making common among composers of modern western classical music, everyone assumes things will remain this way until they become worse which itself is inevitable. Once again sticking his big flabby face in, Debussy watches that chorus of dissent get thicker as it gets louder. Even Schoenberg becomes involved and to everyone's regret.

Bartok returns from wherever he has been, perhaps from death or from one more music conference where his transportation, room and meals all are paid for by some pleasantly fascistic corporation eager to appear less fascistic, even at the risk of appearing pointlessly modern.

There remains a conviction that Bartok knows most of the correct people, including many who are left-handed. There remain gaps where myths involving the nocturnal proclivities and various ignorances of particular modern western classical music composers go to hide. Of these myths, most involve the enemies of those composers attempting to raise their public profiles, attract youthful companionship, but certainly raise money. Bartok snatches at the public eye by wearing a cowboy hat and cowboy boots as if he might convince someone he owns certain cows and particular horses kept at some imaginary ranch optimistic such well-positioned appearance will convince the clueless that all of this could be real. Oddly, audiences accept this silly story at face value, which says something unpleasant about the audience for modern western classical music, unless this is only about Bartok himself.

Never to be outdone in any humiliating attempt to gather public attention, Edgar Varese dresses in feathers, buckskin and beads determined to be misrecognized as an American Indian. He is certain there is a demographic wherein simply wearing the appropriate garb and speaking the appropriate argot will lead to wealth if not happiness. Yet, while their present drifts toward dissolution and rot, none of the composers of modern western classical music, dead or temporarily alive or otherwise, can abandon the delusional fantasy that one day they will be recognized following which they will then be made rich.

Just ask Stravinsky, if any of this still bothers you.

———————

It would prove tedious as well as time-consuming to list all of the composers who pursue certain desperate measures in their climb to what they believe must be fame and fortune or, at the very least, a steady income. But controversy deteriorates into a battle which leaves scars. Yet who among us isn't thrilled at the prospect of a serious music battle? Anticipation sets many a-tremble, especially those who recall the battle between Rossel and Auric with its many injured bystanders.

Ives, meanwhile, once again attempts to perform, "Crystal Rowed the Inflatable Raft Ashore" (composed unfortunately in the Phrygian mode which utterly baffles Ives), on his harmocarina determined that if anyone requests that he play it at the next wedding reception he will be prepared. Privately, Ives regards piano battles as unconscionable wastes of time as well as resources especially considering the frightening loss of pianos. Even worse, those so-called battles corrode the respect and admiration for seriously accomplished piano-warriors. Whenever Ives hears the phrase, 'cultural decline', certain bogus though popular yet brutally destructive piano battles with injured hands and piles of splintered woodwork, come instantly to his mind.

Still, it is Stravinsky who leaves Ives most annoyed, and with the kind of annoyance that works away at the edges of his sleep. But then again, whenever Ives thinks of Prokofiev, instantly he thinks of Shostakovich, and whenever he thinks of Shostakovich, just as immediately, Prokofiev appears before his mind's eye, each very shaggy and dark and smelling unpleasantly. But Stravinsky is and always will be Stravinsky, no matter what Schoenberg or any of the rest of us wishes.

Having conjured a musical antagonism between Alban Berg and Anton Weber, Schoenberg is content that the future of modern western classical music composition is entirely within his own perverted hands and will remain there stinking to high heaven and for as long as he wishes.

And it matters to no one that Poulenc, even if once again dead, has an entirely different idea concerning all of this and prepares to implement it.

Meanwhile, and to the surprise of most, Arthur Honegger returns from death to complete one more of his railroad locomotive symphonies; this one he entitles, "Yellowstone 2-8-8-4".

Along with Auric and Milhaud, Poulenc attempts to gather a musical mob whose dissonances will sound so harmonious they will destroy the market for car commercial jingles. Such ambitions, we note, remain thoroughly French.(Following the banning of commercials to promote the purchase of cigarettes, the arena of car commercials, at least for composers of modern western classical music, explodes resulting in many injuries, albeit hidden and therefore unacknowledged and then easily ignored). Whenever the next music war breaks out, the most urgent question will be who is an ally and who an enemy. Unless the composer in question has allies in at least one or two of the major metropolitan orchestras, every apparent victory will remain empty. Thus, at least in this arena, George Szell in Chicago, Herbert von Karahan in Berlin, Klaus Tennstedt in Vienna, Leonard Bernstein in New York, and of course, Eugene Ormandy in Philadelphia; all under the cloak of darkness embrace the responsibility of keeping modern western classical music obscure and baffling but also noisy and expensive. When any misguided musician attempts to slip in a bit of Brahams or a sliver of Schumann into an evening's performance, the responsibility of these conductors is to assure the work is played badly. Such casual yet determined betrayals must lead to conflicts even among those assumed to be collaborators. But that is still not the worst.

Every performing instrumentalist must eventually become restless. Why, they demand to know, have they spent decades learning the craft of their instrument, only to be compelled to play crap music? Certain among them even threaten to become trick-and-roll musicians, although most agree that in the end a disgruntled musician is more likely to take up some half-baked and barely tolerable genre as obnoxious as jazz-type music, especially since they are doomed to play it awkwardly and half-heartedly and so with unutterable professional embarrassment.

Musicians are compelled to agree that in order to have any career, they must compose and perform furniture music. Milton Babbit, Olivier Messian and even Karl Heinz-Stockhausen admit and acknowledge that the writing has appeared on the wall and so available for everyone to read, especially delusional composers of modern western classical music. Either they embrace the craft of writing furniture music as well as teaching it to the shapeless masses or learn to live without eating. Ives recalls his own attempt to teach the wit-less; its experience lasted nearly fifteen minutes, at the end of which he struck the tow-haired lad before him with a lead baton and then buried his remains in the child's own backyard, a gesture of respect for a talentless brat. But Ives learns his lesson; in a choice between writing furniture music and teaching adolescences, he abandons every hesitation. Even the composition of a jingle for an underarm deodorant offers a grander opportunity for a display of style of which these vicious toddlers are incapable.

With all this Ives is certain things are not about to improve. Besides, he has yet to complete his most recent composition, "All My Cats Are Heathens"; an opera/ballet with feline chorus about a boy cat and a girl cat who wish to marry but their parent-cats refuse to allow it because of cat-religion differences. Ormandy of the Philly-O swears that as soon as Ives finishes the orchestration, he knows who to contact for a chorus of trained singing cats. Always dubious of promises from orchestral conductors, Ives is certain that Ormandy is especially skilled at lying with a straight face. In fact, he hears Ormandy make that same promise to Prokofiev, except that to him he offers a heard of carefully-trained dancing llamas.

The consensus remains that Ormandy is forever several notes short of an octave. The reason so many composers of modern western classical music believe his promises is that so few other conductors bother to accept their phone calls, let alone make the effort to offer impossible-to-believe lies. Whether singing cats or dancing llamas, Ormandy remains oddly sympathetic although never credible and certainly never sufficiently competent.

———————

Meanwhile, Brecht convinces Zubin Meta of the LA Phil to conduct a program of toothpaste jingles composed by Prokofiev and Shostakovich.

There is no confidence among the musicians that such a performance can even be successfully rehearsed, let alone performed, but they decide to keep the flaws of those compositions secret until the last moment since at least they will be paid for their rehearsal time. That secrecy eventually proves impossible to sustain and conductors disagree in a heated fashion, resorting either to attorneys or firearms (never go to a knife-fight without a lawyer). The fact is that choosing a lawyer only underlines the cowardice predictable among conductors as well as composers of modern western classical music.

But the larger issue remains; will anyone tolerate Penderecki's composition of a sonata for glass trombone which he refuses to allow anyone to read, let alone perform, certain that other composers are determined to steal his idea. The possibility, albeit unacknowledged, of a new Hollywood contract sets the hell-hounds of Wall Street panting and drooling and without embarrassment. Milhaud curtails his intrabassoon solos, especially his most famous and popular, his intrabassoon sonata, "Falling Stars Will Find You", a variation on his raucous nightly encore number, "Drooling Idiocy".

So much of modern western classical music composition continues to strike Ives as just fun and games assumed to entertain children. He recalls that at the reformatory, where he takes his first glass trombone lessons, compositions of a particular style and type threaten to descend into musical ambiguity. Later, in the midst of a bout of genital dandruff, he wins that Pork-Pie Award for his opera/ballet, "The Cockamamie Polka," staring several battered Cadillacs driven by poorly-trained monkeys. With this he wonders if his life will soon be surrounded by a thrilling coterie of movie stars and fashion models all of whom will slum for his benefit, certain he has the money to make them happy. Just as it appears his career is about to take off, a local journalist who once knew how to play the drums before forgetting, points out that his previous two ballet/operas, "Why Butterflies Are Not Faries", and "Thank You For Not Caring" are based on the same melody and the same chord changes with only the lyrics and their bag-o-piss rhymes varying between them, and even there not by very much. So what, the journalist asks, is original about repetition?

Brecht asks many of the same questions even while sympathizing with those who struggle to conjure an appropriate response. Like the rest of us, he is prepared to admire that which he will never do.

Having been dismissed as uninteresting, Bartok recognizes he has stumbled into a quagmire of murmurs and mutterings which suggest he learn to play the melophonium, the least likely of instruments to perform modern western classical music, unless it is the baritone intrabassoon. Despite earnest efforts, his collection of intrabasson quartets has somehow proved controversial with all of the cat-calls and brick-bats that accompany and then follow their embattled performers out into the street. Without naming names or making predictions, Bartok suspects that his last performance will prove to be his last performance.

Until recently, the piccolotuba has been exiled from the performance stage and over the intervening centuries few compositions are written for it, and it isn't until Busoni's efforts that the spell is broken. And yet, Bartok's quintets for piccolotuba and trombonophone insistently roil the concert halls around the world, although nowhere more so than Vienna itself. Few composers enjoy writing for such a pathetic instrument ensemble even while that obscurity is the main reason Bartok remains fond of it; like taking up with a dirty and stinking but oddly appealing stray dog. For just that reason, Bartok's name still occasionally appears (inevitably misspelled) in news articles in the journals of modern western classical music composers. Both Shostakovich and Prokofiev remain furiously jealous of even that little attention, even when such notoriety, in addition to whatever curiosity arises, disappears almost instantly. Even Ormandy concludes he should sell his own trombonophone, much to the relief of at least one of his mistresses and all of his neighbors.

When Albert Roussel offers a preview of his newest opera/ballet, "The Crab Nebula Goes Home", there is far more relief than enthusiasm. A complex piece with too many movements, lengthy debate follows its premier in attempts to distinguish the pattern of its music from the sequence of the lyrics. Jean Cocteau is suggested as the arbiter, something he enjoys even while he fails literally to know what he is talking about.

Following being freshly dead, Francise Poulenc appears astride his 1200 cc Harley-Davidson motorcycle doing wheelies before a crowd of motorcycle hysterics. Everyone assumes he will include this noisy din in his next concerto for motorcycle and concert orchestra and with this his audiences are warned thereby.

A rippling mutter of discontent has generalized around the question of whether the sudden proliferation of motorcycle chamber music, including the revving motorcycles, has finally worn out its welcome. At first, all of that noise accompanied by billows of stinking black smoke seems new and bright and revolutionary. But of late, certain voices suggest that such acoustic revisionism is now passe', displaced by regiments of towering loudspeakers beside brooding black and silver amplifiers. Ives ignores this trend as he has done for every other annoying yet inexplicable trend. A consensus is emerging that inclusion of motorcycles as elements of musical compositions and even in certain Broadway shows has indeed been overdone. Critics now deplore regularly the carbon monoxide which is the inevitable result of such obvious attempts at popular appeal even as it shortens the lives of many fine stage-hands as well as the more numerous though not nearly as fine horn players. Of course, the union representing motorcycle musicians is instantly furious just as its members are paying it to be, and threatens a general strike of all motorcycle musicians. Fortunately or unfortunately, few any longer pay attention to motorcycle musicians, even very talented ones.

Bartok knows all of this and secretly even hopes the motorcycle musicians will make good on their threat and go on strike; he still fantasizes an environment where tuned motorcycles once again only concertize in the deepest backwoods and so return live motorcycle music to nature and the masses. After all, it remains one thing to practice the piccolotuba after midnight and something entirely different to be compelled to listen to motorcycles just revving and revving and revving.

Still, when Stravinsky announces his newest work for opera/ballet titled, "Tales of The Wild Sparkplug", promising to be the ultimate composition for motorcycle and whatever other instruments he can compel to apply, there is an obvious boredom resembling annoyance. And yet, this is Stravinsky after all. Motorcycle dealers across the city are queried over which has sold their most recent motorcycle and to whom. The conviction remains that once a last musical composition which includes a motorcycle is performed, a particular chapter in modern western music must close, fortunately for all except the motorcycles and their players.

———

And this is what every other composer of modern western classical music assumes, except for Francise Poulenc who, on a wintry night and over public radio, premieres the love duet for paired motorcycles entitled, "Do You Lie To Your Mother The Way You Lie To Me", a new form of *musique concrete* with the noisy tossing of shovels of gravel and concrete all to the tune of revving motorcycles. Based on the theory of negative projections and irregularly shaped squares the composition combines six different musical scores for the same set of lyrics—each of which then becomes the subject of a copywrite infringement lawsuit involving uninsured motorcycles and their mechanics plus the few musicians who compose for them. With lyrics written by Andre Breton, notorious for his gang of copywrite-lawyer thugs and their numerous and explosive copywrite trials, or so described in the musical press, where armies of knife-wielding attorneys remain both divisive and brutal and leave a trail littered with astonishing court costs and lawyer fees, yet conjure a risible barrel of highly amused monkeys. Modern western classical music remains an unstable market for a panoply of legal mystifications resembling musical/artistic slight-of-hand.

Meanwhile Stravinsky looks around and he just laughs

Ho! Ho! Ho!, Stravinsky laughs, Ho! Ho! ho!

Ives endures the temptation to make one more attempt to raise capital, or at least raise his profile, with a cover feature in Playboy, currently the most authoritative forum scrutinizing modern western classical music. A flattering photograph perhaps that clearly asserts his status as a composer of modern western classical music capable of discomforting perspectives on modern western classical music and its composition as well as possessor of a remarkably effective phallus. Much money must then arise to drift relentlessly but certainly toward him. But when he hears the melody Copeland submits for his own profile, several current projects no longer seem very much fun. And then startled by the melody Schoenberg submits, Ives remembers the pamphlet he keeps in his desk drawer for that plumbing school offering a full scholarship for depressed composers of modern western classical music covering all six years plus a poorly paying internship accompanied by vague assistance in his job search if he continues on to that Ph. D.

Charles Ives recognizes that he will soon need to find useful work since the royalties for his most recent opera/ballet, "The Short Guy Rides Shotgun", whose theme of a cowboy and a cowgirl who fall in love and decide to marry but their horses refuse their approval since the cowboy is too short leading to mutual despair sprinkled with ecstasy and much bawdy humor (late in the performance the dancers sing as they dance and gradually disappear). More urgently he begins work on a ballet/opera entitled "The Graveyard of Gravity" for eight dancing singers and whose premise is that an overabundance of silence led to Beethoven's deafness, a danger the twentieth century goes far toward eradicating. Schoenberg is queried about all this and insists Beethoven's story here leaves out all of the sexy parts. But soon it becomes universal in modern western classical music performance that all the singers of a ballet/opera must dance and all of the dancers must sing.

The difficulty, as Ives agrees, is the cost of the elephants and whether they should hire more or fewer than Prokofiev has for his ballet/opera titled "Jumbo Is No Dumbo", about a boy and a girl who live under a glass dome and hope to marry but are refused and so the glass dome becomes fogged with steam completely obscuring their urgent efforts at unsanctioned intimacy. Ives reluctantly prepares to modify this composition since at an earlier rehearsal the dancing elephants cause a sudden collapse of the stage and end up in a court case which will be impossible to settle within any person's lifetime and also will cost tons.

Despite certain challenges Ives remains fond of this albeit uneven work and even adds a percussion solo of smashing together of a dozen drinking glasses as an element of humor. For this he experiments to find that precisely crystalline sound of the shattering clatter of ordinary glasses which in no way resembles that distinctive tinkle of glittering crystal glasses. With all of this, Ives finds himself as annoyed as he is reassured.

The new conductor at the Houston Symphony Orchestra writes to Ives a very large check for the performance of a piece Ives composed in music school entitled, "The Ziggurats of Pompeii". But to his fury, that check bounces after Ives has already sent the score thereby reminding him once again that orchestral conductors must never be trusted, particularly in the exchange of music for money.

Otherwise and at nearly the same time, Arthur Honegger completes what he believes is his most ambitious and wide-ranging railroad locomotive symphony which he entitles, "Pennsylvania 6-4-4-6".

Across town, Milhaud, surprisingly returned from the dead, continues to apply to various movie studios confident that, with Stravinsky's success at Disney, eventually these studios will be eager for his services. But only M-G-M makes an offer and while it appears substantial, he is expected to compose music for their Mike and Yike cartoons, which never even make Milhaud smile, even when he is more drunk than dead.

And there remains Bartok. Having lusted for months after Poulenc's Harley-Davidson and failing to get even close, he plots for a way to afford a Triumph, one of those very big, heavy ones from big and heavy England. He is certain he has ridden his very last Japanese bike, tired of the tinny sound and flimsy construction. Japanese bikes are quick off the mark and can zip along, but don't climb any hills or find bumps in front of you unless your health insurance is paid up. Besides, after a while they begin to smell funny and not in a ha-ha way. Ironically, even Bartok is ready to turn from Japan to England and not look back.

What Ives also keeps in mind is that Hindemith has sold his complete Kammermusik to Disney and for a very large sum of money. Each part will be expanded to provide background music to a new cartoon series in development which stars a lively and charming cockroach of significant size named Konrad and who sings and dances just like Charlie Chaplin.

Ives learns that Stravinsky has signed a lucrative contract with a particularly famous circus to write dance music for their lions and tigers; prancing lions and waltzing tigers suddenly and inexplicably are the rage. This contract does not appeal to Stravinsky since he prefers to write music for clowns and their thigh-slapping hijinks, but this circus has also signed a separate contract with Prokofiev, thus leaving Stravinsky certain they plan to compare scores as if in some lottery. Stravinsky manages to dispose of this request by tossing off an unimaginative melody based on the chord changes to the old folk tune entitled, "The Windshield Wipers of Love". Predictably, the Society for the Preservation of Future Anomalies initiates a lawsuit claiming cultural spoliation and demanding a remarkably large amount of money for just three minutes of music. It should be noted that this lawsuit will continue in litigation until well beyond the final demise of all of the parties immediately involved, named or merely referenced.

Soon after, Tristan Tzara acquires a job restocking shelves at the local music store, and while this new job is nowhere near ideal, especially as he risks damage to his otherwise delicate piano-playing hands, its schedule of work between eleven pm and four thirty am leaves the rest of the day for him to—in some order—get drunk, write music and rehearse his band (this latest he calls Nirvana Sucks). And then to the surprise of most, Prokofiev and Shostakovich break up their own band (recording as Erotic Tension) announcing their decision to go separate ways and finally write the music each has repressed due to the presence of the other; occasions like this occur often in modern western classical music but are rarely resolved without gun-play.

———————

Then, and so quickly that one assumes it is finished before their band breaks up, Erotic Tension releases what appears a monstrous hit single titled, "Pardon Me Boys, Is That The Eiffel Tower?" Aimed at that increasingly elderly WW II crowd, it premiers in the music charts at number seven but after just a week it tops the charts and with a bullet remaining there for nearly six weeks and proving to be so popular that Disney titles a new animated feature after it. But as is inevitable, barely scrupulous composers decide to cash-in with their own covers. Within a week Milhaud, still recovering from being dead along with his new band, Booty Sleep, releases their own cover titled, "Pardon Me Boys, Is That The Planet Saturn?" Refusing to be outdone, Schoenberg, preforming with his new band, Digital Disaster, pens the ditty, "Pardon Me Boys, Is That Another Asshole?", which instantly threatens to take over the number one slot. And with this the greed machine cranks up to eleven. Reluctant to be left behind when there is so much obvious money lying about, Edgar Varese with his new band, Box Of Funnybones, conjures, "Pardon Me Boys, Is That Another Drum Solo?" The tornado of rip-offs expands, and hot on their heels, Poulenc tosses off, "Pardon Me Boys, Is That An Onion Bagel?" in one more attempt to squeeze some cash from a desperately withered phenomenon and in the process adding an utterly inappropriate and totally unnecessary tessitura. Meanwhile and despite money recently paid by MGM, Hindemith scribbles the cleverly amusing, "Pardon Me Boys, Is That A Graphite Pencil?", adding one more extension to a shriveling phenomenon. And finally, always late to every party, Auric pushes out the vaguely embarrassing, "Pardon Me Boys, Is That The Way To San Jose?" Since the title scans poorly, it attracts less money than disdain.

But the challenge for all composers of modern western classical music remains the same; how to turn musical notes into bank notes. Ravel and Debussy each insist on a fool-proof formula that showers them with desirables yet no one duplicates their humiliating success. Auric tries to be satisfied writing music for movies that will never be made assuming rarity assures attention. But given the pathetic greed of Hollywood with its billowing, drifting, smothering clouds of unassigned money, getting paid is the last thing anyone assumes.

––––––––––

Ferruccio Busoni and Erik Satie resume writing music to accompany Pablo Picasso's most recent play, "Tell Me Again Why You Hate Me", a story about a boy painter and a girl sculptor who fall in love and wish to marry but their gallery director refuses to allow it, certain that otherwise he will make less money. Following the success of Picasso's previous comedy, "Thank You For Not Laughing", a play in which a boy comedian and a girl comedian fall in love and announce that they intend to marry and are then greeted with guffaws of laughter, critics agree that he is on a roll and everything he touches turns into something less foul-smelling than gold.

At this point in their careers, Satie and Busoni need this to be the case and in fact must bank on it. Especially since their last joint composition, "No Harm, No Foul," the story of a boy football player and a girl football player who fall in love and decide to marry but their coach refuses to allow it since it will make the other players want to marry and that will let down the team, which one must never do, has proved a disaster with patrons fleeing the stadium even before the end of the first quarter, especially the Spanish-speaking audiences since, in translation, the title appears to read "Lovely Rita, Ya Can't Beat 'Ah". While this expression is not regarded as blasphemous, it comes too close for certain sensibilities.

Still, when Poulenc finishes his first compilation album entitled "More Beans Than Franks", he is finally recognized as a composer who commands the attention of that critical 18-to-80 year-old demographic, something that can be said about hardly any other composer of modern western classical music.

Meanwhile, Hindemith discovers that his Kammermusik, sold to Disney for a very large sum of money, will instead provide the background to a cartoon series staring Ever-Stephen, a large and lively but also endearing red and blue striped caterpillar of a certain size who sings and dances in ways that resemble Charlie Chaplin (development of this project has gone on for what seems an eternity and without promise of a completion date).

In effect, these composers of modern western classical music appear finally, even if momentarily, to have achieved some elevated visibility, thereby offering false hope and fraudulent optimism to many baffled colleagues practicing invisibly and profitlessly within the profession.

This gesture of vacuous encouragement proves disastrous to those who, out of an overabundance of optimism, max out their credit cards certain they are about to be offered all the capital needed to cover the accumulating expenses of drugs and alcohol and erotic companionship, thereby demonstrating, if such is needed, that composers of modern western classical music are even more thoughtlessly self-absorbed than the rest of us.

Ives attempts to find his footing among these distractions and false leads. Even more broke than he has ever been, he recognizes he is surrounded by composers of modern western classical music far wealthier than he will ever be while composing the crappiest music he has ever refused to allow to enter his ears.

———————

At about this time, Samuel Beckett publishes his most popular self-help volume entitled, "How To Be Who You Are When You're Not Feeling Yourself". Following the sale of its movie rights for an astonishing amount of money, the rumor of a musical version for the stage of an unnamed city sets tongues wagging, albeit in all the wrong directions.

Ives can ill-afford to ignore these swirling rumors and considers offering his own submission, if only to insist that others recognize his contributions to modern western classical music. But he also knows he must compete with drunken and smelly Russians. Still, given the visibility of this project and the money, he must at least put in an appearance.

In the midst of these competitions, Bartok, who at this point is so broke he sleeps on Prokofiev's couch, breaks up his old band (The Tag-Team Heros, as you'll recall) and in its place forms a quintet (The Tag-Team Heros Plus One). In anticipation of certain collaborations, he announces his completion of a group of thirteen brief glass trombone quintets he entitles "Capriccio For You Know Who Doing You Know What". He is pessimistically certain he will fail to snag a single contract but he loathes being ignored. Antoine Artaud, on the other hand, is frantically buying up second-hand doors in order to complete his latest film, "Gods Without Doors"; comprised of a series of short films about doors but photographed in different primary colors (his most recent is titled, "Blue-Eyed Redheads And Their Vampires"). Unsurprisingly, Artaud finds the money for this even while he still owes Ives quite a bit and without thought of repayment.

Meanwhile, George Braque remains pissed off at Picasso for having purloined his most recent mistress, Eleanora Argentina, known to the modeling world as Kathy Smith. This insult inspires a new composition for orchestra, chorus, and multiple four-wheel vehicles entitled "Quadrupeds With Corvairs", a story in which a boy compact car and a girl compact car fall in love but their mechanic refuses to allow them to marry and sends the boy compact car to the re-cyclers, all accompanied by peals of raucous laughter. A sensitive and moving work, it is dedicated to the memory of all those who have lost their lives while watching movies; the sense of loss within the film-making community remains broadly felt if millimeters deep.

Charles Ives scratches his head over these utterly baffling movie music compositions and their dim-witted but lucrative contacts. And here he is not alone. Even to composers bothered by the explosion of compositions written to accompany explosions on screen, this blizzard of contracts appears without thought or limit. Ives would appreciate Milhaud's consultation, but he is once again dead. Ives warmly recalls a time when one could get by composing music to accompany various forms of dance, even including wheelchair basketball. After all, so many have done so little for so few.

———————

But dances are more than sufficient to stimulate him to write music responsive to their demand. Roussel however confesses his own abhorrence of dance, tracing it back to his infancy when his mother is frightened by misdirected belly-dancer. Whereas, Ives cannot help himself and continues to write music for a few aberrant terpsichoreans. His best guess is that changing popular tastes must eventually eviscerate the so-called movie industry, while ballet/opera in the form of show-and-tell tunes will degenerate into an odious form of light operetta. But with this conclusion, he wonders how he and composers like him writing the music they do, despite the crosswinds and depressions which swirl everywhere, will manage to cash-in. This question remains fundamental; how to cash in, in order to cash out.

When production of Henry Miller's most recent opera/ballet, "Excrement Become Nutrient," begins final rehearsal, Shostakovich claims the score for the dance is complete, whereas Miller includes no dance numbers since the ballet concerns a boy oak tree and a girl pine tree who fall in love but foresters cut them down to be made into toothpicks (surprisingly, Shostakovich relents composing a happy ending where, in a later and fiscally responsible revision, the wood of the boy oak tree is made into a bed-frame and the wood of the girl pine tree is made into a chest of drawers and they remain together occupying the same bedroom until a fire reduces them to charred hulks—so typical of a Russian to find this ending happy).

Predictably, the uproar over Miller's so-called opera/ballet is instantaneous. Just as unsurprisingly, Prokofiev is the loudest if not the first to ask how a score can be written for an opera/ballet that has no dance. Shostakovich insists the music is composed while conjuring dance-like images as choreography appropriate to Miller's words. Even Stravinsky laughs, mostly because he has claimed this same technique for years. Besides, Stravinsky laughs at everything and everyone but especially Charles Ives. Hearing this, Milhaud, now returned to life, becomes darkly furious since he has scored several of Miller's earlier opera/ballets and should have had a right of first refusal. But Allan Ginsberg, Miller's combative and heroin-addicted theatrical agent, pounds the negotiating table with his shoe that Miller's work will never go merely to the highest bidder, but only to the most enthusiastic conductor, or who Miller decides has the sexiest wife (embarrassment remains universal concerning Miller's tastes and how he satisfies them, but their exercise is the least likely of his personal habits to cost him money—besides, confinement within a prison remains an option).

Otherwise and unnoticed by the musical press, Arthus Honegger premiers his most recent, and surprisingly popular railroad locomotive symphony and this one with chorus, titled "Adriatic 2-6-4".

———————

Conditions among composers of modern western classical music deteriorate, especially for those who compose symphonies; costs inflate and the price of rehearsing a performance involving even ten players cripples all but the wealthiest composers while the price of competent drummers goes through the proverbial roof. And paying someone to play the intrabassoon? Even you, dear reader, can't have that kind of money. The only music that still covers its costs of performance is solo banjo; banjoists being the most despised musicians aside from accordionists, and so inevitably the most desperate and therefore grateful for even minimal payment. As for those still insufficiently skilled or desperate enough to compose banjo music for commercials advertising arthritis medicines, grants-in-aid are available although in the past these grants have been directed to the love-children of occasionally dead but still notorious banjoists even when their music is no longer modern (embarrassment within the community of composers rarely proves unbearable). It is pointed out that these love-children almost never compose, practice or perform on the banjo, but this corruption continues since impropriety is never an excuse but merely a condition, and even then, easily ignored.

———————

The highlight of the upcoming music season, as everyone agrees, is the premier of Arron Copeland's newest folk/ballet/opera, "Thank You For Being Nobody", the story of a boy farmer and a girl farmer who decide to marry but their farm animals revolt and refuse to allow it after which hilarious agricultural mayhem ensues. Largely because Copeland's most recent work, "We Came For The Sunshine", has proved a financial disaster, even Jack Kerouac in his review published in a Evergreen Magazine, which occasionally pays him, fails to disguise its embarrassment. In a baffling essay, he decries the "perverted ambitions" of modern western classical music, complaining that no one can even whistle their tunes while their rhythms remain impossible for the average working person to count. How can it be music, he asks rhetorically, if you can't tap your foot to it or at least sing the harmony parts in the shower? Ives refuses to admire Kerouac as a music critic but occasionally he values his urgency, albeit misguided, in his determination to promote music he misunderstands but usually finds at least mildly amusing.

But spring returns, and with it, announcements of the upcoming season's awards. As always, Ives attempts to remain above this particular mental confetti, but to his regular embarrassment he knows that in the end, with teeth firmly clenched and nauseous with fury, he will watch talentless children be awarded more money in one evening than he possesses in all of his secret bank accounts.

Brecht, meanwhile, has one more argument with Schoenberg, and this time nothing Pierre Boulez adds makes things better. Boulez secretly has encouraged Schoenberg to submit a score for Raymond Queneau's latest comedic drama, "Parallax Is A Point Of View", a heart-wrenching story of a boy bodybuilder and a girl bodybuilder who fall in love and decide to marry but their physiotherapist refuses to allow it, certain that marriage will cause their perfect bodies to inflate and then deteriorate. What sets Brecht wondering is the score composed by Boulez which he submits for Guillaume Apollinaire's cantata, "How Quickly We Reappear", a work for eighteen non-dancing singers and a piccolotuba quintet based on a Hindu text of great antiquity that has become popular campus reading.

Knowing recording executives as he does, Brecht is determined to remain current with the youth while also spying on his contemporaries. These efforts are regularly as pointless as they are profitless since the work he must consider invariably sucks marbles. But then, if no one actually cares, who can be left to care? Yet total discouragement remains rare for an artist like Ives, and is even occasionally exhilarating as long as it is depressing.

Because, to his relief, it still happens that, upon hearing a piece of new music, Ives suddenly finds himself as excited as he was as a teenager.

The smell of gunpowder, the sight of warm flesh, the sound of clashing armor, fade to nothing compared to a stage packed with inept, poorly-paid and sweating musicians; this still sets him to tremble. Because he knows well that genuinely new work always pisses off somebody since it regularly fails to be old. And Brecht works as hard as any of his contemporaries to make his music sound old regardless of how new it is, and so acquires the slimmest of possibilities of being heard, no matter how irritating such music often proves to be.

So when Brecht hears about the new cycle of folk dances that is Stravinsky's most recent contribution to modern western classical music, entitled, "Uglier Than You Are", about a charming prince who refuses to kiss the ugly princess in three acts and written in a style which enchants teenage women, he trembles; perhaps modern western classical music is truly coming to an end!

But then again, how bad could that be?

On the topic of teenage women, who has forgotten Richard Wagner's determined attempts in the last century to bring modern western classical music to its knees, and how close he came? So confident of his success that all through the premier of "Scheherazade" by Rimsky-Korsakov, he laughs, cackles and howls hysterically. Those two guys, he insists to everyone within hearing, know even less about music than I do.

As discouraged as Ives feels about the future of modern western classical music, he remains relieved when his recording label finally releases a series of jingles he composes to promote a credit card that offers lending rates at less than some others. Ives has very little money which he keeps in a brown paper bag hidden inside his upright piano. So few are curious anymore about how to play the piano, Ives is certain his money is safe.

Despite distractions from Stravinsky, Shostakovich attempts to make his own large even if subtle splash with the sound-track for a new movie scored for Joan Miro Studios entitled, "The Fortress Of Latitude," about a mad scientist who turns gold into dirt and thereby threatens the global financial system which then triggers something to resemble the end of the world, more or less and sort of. Ives finds the film not as bad as it looks.

But Ravel and Debussy make their own plans. Managing to escape a suffocating contract with RCA, they form their own company, R & D Studios. Debussy insists it be called D & R Studios and they argue so long and loud they're compelled to flip a coin, a gesture neither approves of as something that Dumb-Dumb John Cage does and imagines himself clever. On the other hand, at paper-rock-scissors Ravel almost always wins, so this is likely the most equitable way to settle their dispute.

The first composer their new recording company signs is none other than Francise Poulenc. And they feel particularly fortunate as he completes his most recent composition, a ballet/opera entitled "The Otherness Of The Other", where a strange boy and a strange girl who are very different fall in love but are unable to marry because they are so very different. The lead singer/dancer is Glenn Gould fresh from his recent exile resulting from his recording of a high school marching band, his best effort at a cross-over recording. Unfortunately this angers many fans of high school marching band music feeling betrayed by the duplicitous arrogance of one more bourgeois intellectual whose pretentions pervert our high schools and their never-innocent students. Yet despite blistering letters to the editor, Gould manages to sing-and-dance his way back into the hearts of many loyal even if baffled Canadians.

Milhaud, having completed the score for, "The Big Red Thing Goes For A Walk", a documentary film concerning a big, red thing that moves from place to place for no discernable reason, finds none of this amusing. Having forfeit one more dispatcher's job with his most recent death, he is in a near-panic that his grant from the Honorable Foundation for Broke Composers will fail to arrive; he promises each of his girlfriends at least that much although his landlord remains among the most pissed-off when said checks fail to arrive. Milhaud is certain this all has something to do with Schoenberg; there is no level of mischief to which that man will not descend. If anything, it is his certainty about all of this which remains among the few regularities reassuring him and thus keeping him vaguely sane.

————

A surprisingly long month elapses before Stravinsky drops a new recording so that the world of composers of modern western classical music wonders if he has recently been dead even briefly. But that world does not need to consider the question for very long. On New Year's Eve, the Globe Theater throws open its doors for the premier of the epic film, "Abigail and the Butt-less Wonders", scored by Stravinsky himself, obviously no longer dead. Produced in three parts, Stravinsky composes a separate score for each. Soon after its disastrous premier and quoted in an interview in Car and Driver Magazine,

Stravinsky confesses that, honestly, the book he is handed to score is simply too long to be read by any human being who is not dead and so feels no obligation to read it. He confesses that in fact he has no idea what the book is about and so does nothing with it beyond using it as an excuse to spoil stacks of perfectly clean and white sheets of paper with tiny black dots. Yet he remains grateful to Walt Disney for the checks being sent to him along with that charming pet sea lion which attempts to bite him whenever it sees him (the checks just cover the cost of cans of sea lion food).

Meanwhile, reduced as usual to plotting and scheming, Milhaud returns from being dead determined to promote his six septets for intrabassoon quartet and industrial vacuum cleaner entitled "The Skeleton's Funeral". Despite glowing reviews, the collection goes nowhere commercially. More than a few of its reviews insist the work highlights the industrial vacuum cleaner as an inspiration for a whole new chapter to characterize modern western classical music for the rapidly approaching twenty-first century. Yet sales for each of the septets remain dismal, if any are ever sold at all. But the conviction among the knowledgeable remains that this annoying new music and its controversy challenges honest reviewers to identify any music that is newer. Following an acrimonious meeting with recording company executives, Milhaud's manager (Vachel Linsey replaces Carl Sandburg sentenced to seven years with three more tacked on for his horrid reviews) describes to him a host of ancillary charges slathered over by his current contract insisting these unpaid charges are the real reason he earns no money (never let it be said that being dead is cheap).

Or so Milhaud's new business manager insists.

Although they have never liked each other and their music is so different, Satie agrees with Milhaud that he is being ripped-off and that his manager and his music publisher but especially those recording company executives must be stealing as much of his money as they can find. Albeit briefly and in passing, Satie mentions the word 'lawyer' but then seeing the expression on Milhaud's face instantly regrets the obvious mistake and laughs in embarrassment. Thus, at what many in the music industry agree is the nadir of Milhaud's career, he pens the first few notes of the opening of what becomes among the most well-known in the world of grand ballet/opera, "Why Should I Do You A Favor?", the story of a rich boy and a poor girl who fall in love and plan to marry but both of their respective fathers refuse claiming that not enough money will change hands let alone enter an escrow account. The composition demands two more years for its completion, followed by six months of rehearsals and revisions before its grand premier, an evening that none in the musical world will ever forget (the body count following the battle outside the concert hall has never been exceeded). The baton for that performance is wielded by none other than Pierre Monteux, ironically the conductor of the only other premier whose body-count, bloody fights and belittling name-calling accompanied by irritating whining, approaches Milhaud's piece, and that is the premier of Stravinsky's comic but odoriferous opera/ballet, "Tales of The Farting Irish", in which a boy football player and a girl football player fall in love and decide to marry but due to certain gastric disturbances discover that marriage is beyond them and must be abandoned just as they approach their goal line.

––––––––––

Ives is determined to keep up with developments in modern western classical music, and events like premiers along with frustrating recording sessions and interminable alcoholic lunches with rapacious company executives claim his attention until they distract him from completing his own compositions, many of which now lay disguised as fist-sized balls of crumpled white paper scattered across his floor. Still, he begins each day eager to advance one or another of these tattered, abandoned and incomplete works.

He hopes his attention to the works of others will deflect a despair concerning his own. Unable to begin his own composition career until he passes thirty years of age, he does whatever he needs in order to catch up. Despite furious curiosity and urgent determination, he endures an intense sense of inferiority and thus a desperation to surpass his contemporaries. Indeed, he recognizes a gap separating him from all those others pretending to compose music in this most modern idiom. He remembers attending music school sitting beside students fortunate to grow up with a piano or some more primitive form of keyboard in their homes, just as he envies kids who grow up with a pool table or a ping-pong table in their basements but especially those kids whose fathers teach them to play various, invariably unpleasant and sweaty and even painful sports. Raised in a baffled part of the country, it isn't until Ives meets Wallace Stevens in high school that he finds someone to encourage his enthusiasm for music composition. Lately in contact with composers who's works he listens to with respectful admiration, he fails to convince himself his compositions, despite enthusiasm directed toward his work by others, are worthy of such attention. The odd thing is that even Brecht praises almost as often as he criticizes Ives' compositions, as if prepared to encourage Ives but only just enough. So Ives is grateful for Satie's support just as he is certain that Stravinsky will eagerly put a lit match to anything Ives writes.

––––––––––

Prokofiev and Shostakovich remain large and smelly and argue relentlessly, yet they agree that Stravinsky and his noisy music are contemptable just as they remain unanimous in their annoyance with Ives and his work. Regardless of all of this, once he makes his deal with Disney, Hindemith becomes the focus for a wave of envious abuse resembling the exclusive domain of Richard Wagner. The fact remains that if there is one composer who draws near-universal contempt and derision from every thinking composer of modern western classical music, Wagner remains the one. Certainly it is conceded he might conjure a clever tune and his orchestrations occasionally appear nearly interesting even if in an unlikely way, in the end it is agreed he is an over-fed half-wit with just enough musical education to conjure charming failures. All of this provides ribald humor involving questions concerning his several mistresses and whether they actually belong to him or if he rents them from Brahams or even simply recruits them from the local Girl Scouts. Making as much sense as he can manage, Hindemith ignores the envy of other musicians when that effort so consumes his concentration and thus distracts him from composing that he considers either changing his manager or hiring a new lawyer.

But in the end he agrees with every other composer of modern western classical music, this is all really about Schoenberg.

––––––––––

Due to his vast wealth, Schoenberg gathers a small coterie of unconscionably mediocre and dull composers of modern western classical music, and with them establishes a corporation for the methodical formulation, copywriting and distribution of furniture music. The intention is to offer musical distraction to the most powerful corporations also possessing the deepest pockets. His job is to compose music which, once heard, crouches down within a human ear causing customers as well as employees to feel delighted with themselves, their environment and particularly their work as either customers or employees for which they are rewarded, all for the greed of certain pitiless corporate overlords, their viciousness and brutality. The anthems that result are then broadcast through the corporation's public address system along with various radio stations in order to distract each employee or customer who hears it. Composing these anthems, Schoenberg and his crew draw from ancient folk-melodies along with various antiquated yet familiar dances and sing-alongs. These collaborators assume that folk-melodies draw on images and emotions buried deep within each employee's or customer's subconscious and their stimulation will prove infectious and even irresistible. Schoenberg expects to charge these corporate entities such unconscionably huge amounts of money that they will consider a bankruptcy while allowing him to pay his confederates and their vociferous mistresses well and often.

Needless to say, all of this faithless greed drives Milhaud nuts and he cannot decide whether to argue or return to being dead. He is compelled to recognize the level of corruption at the heart of modern western classical music. His own fury just barely contained, he tries to enlist either Prokofiev or Shostakovich in his crusade. But each time they seem about to agree, suddenly they offer urgent pleas concerning how deeply broke they are and even compete over which is more broke than the other. But the choppy waters of modern western classical music composition roil and churn threatening to cast up more half-witted composers attempting some precedent-shattering and therefore boring work of composition.

Certain that they know a better way, Auric and Varese spend months living on a farm in a secret location in someone's mountains working to complete their newest composition, an all-singing, all-dancing Halloween extravaganza entitled, "Sappho vs. Frankenstein". Scored for twenty mixed instruments and another eighteen percussionists (for Varese, one can never have too many drummers) these also include six marimba players and four conga players. The composition offers the story of a boy-monster named Sappho and a girl ballet-dancer named Frankenstein who fall in love despite their deep differences in background, education, physical constitution and permanently attached limbs and also the refusal of their parent's permission. As is otherwise well-known, such conditions are, for every lover, that necessary prelude to desperate, baffled, guilt-ridden and so inevitably hilarious sex. Auric insists this story is his invention although others point out its uncanny similarity to a tale included in James Joyce's collection of stories entitled, "Ulysses" (Disney's most recent acquisition as a graphic novel soon to be made into another uninteresting movie).

To his credit, Auric resists every criticism with energy, but the Musician's Union along with the Pipefitters Local (despite his occasional musical success, Joyce keeps his pipefitters union membership dues up to date certain that regardless of any current success, one never knows the future, do one) insist they will defend their brother pipe-fitter's copyright as well as all artistic prerogatives. Thus, when Anton Weber demands that his contribution to their project be acknowledged with a royalty check, it is pointed out to him that his total contribution amounts to the movement of one single comma. His retort, unremarkably, is that the movement of that comma results in an entirely unique composition, as if that argument has the slightest chance in front of a copywrite judge.

Unfortunately, this ludicrous attitude is adopted by Karl Heinze Stockhausen who rails against the obvious contempt with which certain dim-witted non-musicians regard such a claim. Something of a scandal threatens involving certain dancers who are also members of a rival pipe-fitters local. At issue is whether either the singers or the dancers are musicians and should be paid as such and union representatives are nearly as indifferent as they are unclear.

As usual for Brecht, the question boils down to an intriguing but obscure distinction which even Stravinsky must concede on those frequent at-home evenings when he huddles among his mistresses counting his money. The issue appears to be; should the amount of money a person is paid be based on the immediate effect of their performance, or the time and effort of training that performance demanded, or instead, the likelihood a stranger will voluntarily hand over a sum of money to witness that performer's performance. Brecht attempts to account for even the least important distinction since he intends to acquire the most justifiable compensation if not also the largest. Musicians, he constantly hears, are never paid what they are worth let alone what their education and training demand.

But the music business continues to churn in a terrifying flux occasionally even resulting in bloodshed.

Finding that his motorcycle needs the cylinders rebored and gear-box reconditioned, Satie recognizes that checks of large denominations fly about like mosquitos refusing to land, and also like mosquitos prove impossible to snare on the wing. Even Prokofiev has ideas about the relationship between performance, training and compensation. Having spent years attempting to teach music to teen-agers, he knows he has never been paid for what he has endured. A path of bitterness spreads before him posted among wasted and dissipated opportunities which, had they been pursued, would have propelled him to the top of every list of composers, after which he would have been paid a lot more money.

In fact, it isn't Satie himself or even his motorcycle that stimulates this challenge, but Satie's wife, Martha, who complains hourly that he never takes her anywhere interesting or fun and never buys her anything really nice, unlike Varese's wife, also named Martha and possessor of a vastly different appetite but otherwise thrills at her position and her acquisitions. On occasions when Satie remembers to be even slightly generous to Martha, his Martha, he must admit he could do better and probably he should. Certainly he always brings her along when he goes out for an evening to shoot pool, or when Satie gives some performance somewhere of something, unless it is someone else performing one of his compositions. And yet he admits that even Stravinsky is more thoughtful and generous to his most recent wife, Evita, as well as his several sequentially rotating mistresses. And hasn't Stravinsky just recently written an opera/ballet for Evita to sing as well as giving her name as its title? As he thinks of it, Satie wonders if he should write his own ballet/opera dedicated to his own Martha celebrating all of the crossword puzzles she has solved while waiting for Satie to finish writing one more goofy and profitless piece of modern western classical music or else finish another rack of pool. Musicians or mistresses; it is always about compensating someone for something.

In fact, Satie expects to earn so much money writing modern western classical music that eventually he will never again need to write music for money, but instead he will raise roses fulltime. And if in some future he becomes curious about music again, he will simply turn on his radio since there, someone is always playing something even if it is never Satie's music.

Of course, the other Martha, Vares's wife, considers this aspiration just less corrosive than poison. In the back of her mind she nurses a plan that if Satie will simply leave his Martha to her own devices, her boredom will overwhelm her until she flees the world of modern western classical music for something with a more hot-house yet off-beat twang. In her mind Martha reaches that point quickly, agreeing to run off with her current secret lover, unremarkably named Angelo, a union electrician who, unknown to this Martha, plays glass trombone on the weekend as opposed to seahorse racing wherein several times he has nearly drown. Besides, she would never be caught dead raising anything as common as roses; just so much like a cliché on steroids.

Shostakovich and Prokofiev hint to mutual friends that they have engaged in certain communications, and a suggestion begins to circulate that they are each considering putting their old band (called The Baffled Jesuits) back together. Many of their conversations involve nostalgia and sentiment and the burden of misperception along with certain amounts of money even though such mistakes trigger their first enthusiasms and therefore will eventually dissolve, stripped of that which has gone before even while it may happen again. And yet nothing is ever as simple as that.

Among such discussions, Prokofiev assures Shostakovich that he will work up new tunes as well as revise the charts for some of their old ones, determined to convince Shostakovich there's enough material for at least two albums, but that with both of them at work they will have enough material to release a double-album of Christmas music just in time for the next holiday.

But questions concerning spouses and performance merely lead to more questions involving other spouses and other performances. It is an established fact impossible to ignore; composers of modern western classical music remain especially unfortunate when it comes to finding genuinely hot dates. And this despite the fact, universally affirmed, that composers of modern western classical music make more money than they ever have before; unfortunately not a lot more and probably only just slightly more. Still, for any and all clever enough and determined enough to compose modern western classical music and so link their fate to some wealthy corporate entity, there will always be money. Where and in what direction this money drifts, fantasies explode like fireworks in a summer sky. Among the sundry spousal-style units, such fantasies take on distinctive material shape along with a profundity of dimension possessing an aroma all their own.

Happily ignorant of all of this, Poulenc steps from his front door, certain that today finally he will be paid what he is owed. In fact, he has just completed a new ballet/opera entitled, "Nonexistence Is Futile", which he expects to sell to Aaron Copeland who will then retitle it "The Peculiar Carelessness of the Elderly" and then pass it off as his own work. For too long Poulenc composes his music with the assumption he will never be paid what he is truly worth so he rationalizes his sale to Copeland wondering whether anyone is getting paid what they are worth. He has no doubt that some are paid more than they are worth, whereas—and of this Poulenc is certain—so many others are being paid less, if they are paid anything at all. With that, the real challenge is to make do with what you are paid despite everything else because regardless of what you do, you will never be paid enough to make whatever you do worth doing.

Auric, on the other hand, being an inveterate gambler, refuses to see things this way, and through that attitude the rat races continue to benefit.

———

Beginning in his youth, Auric is assured he must always be prepared to fight for more because there is no such thing as enough. More than last time, more than anyone else, more than anything else, he is assured that whatever he doesn't get someone else will. He will then fail to get all of whatever it is he deserves let alone expects. Music, especially modern western classical music, is so much like this that contradiction evaporates. Just sprinkle lots of black dots over a sheet of clean white paper and then sit back while the money pours in through every opening in your otherwise shabby and trivial existence.

At least that is how it is promised to Georges Auric.

Even at graduate music school, instructor after professor insists that with their highly-effective training, within just a few decades following a begrudging graduation, he will become nearly as rich as his instructors. For better or worse, Auric believes all they promise since a professor would never lie to him. What, after all, could be the point to that? He reminds himself that they are old and deeply experienced and there is no point to any of them fooling him.

But Prokofiev recognizes that the more musicians, the less work for any single one. So why would anyone attempt to convince him, or anyone, that happiness comes from staring at a page of white paper covered with tiny black dots? Prokofiev hesitates, no longer certain he has even a rough idea of the totality of this crisis which appears to be gathering around him like a drift of fallen leaves. Such confusion clouds Prokofiev's days, especially when the hour has grown late. He rarely has enough money to cover his dinner; one more tale told to him by one more idiot with one more musical instrument in hand. Besides and as everyone knows, two lies never make a truth; at least that is what John Cage insists although always with a loud laugh.

Brecht knows as much of all this as he wishes to know in order to know enough to not want to know any more. There are times when certain questions lead to unlikely answers, or at least a range of undesirable responses. An adequate number of answers must accompany every question. Prokofiev knows all this much better than most other composers.

So when Stravinsky's newest opera/ballet, composed in psychodialectric sonorities and titled "Drumline Torment", premiers, the public and critical response is even quieter than silence. As the love story of a beautiful drum majorette and an ugly drummer whose percussive dissonances prevent them from finding the beat, it develops that the most remarkable element of this new opera/ballet is how few people show up to endure it; as if indifference is a new although dispiriting subgenre of approval, as if to assert that this music sounds so good nobody needs to hear it. Unless this musical category is so subtle it becomes its own sub-subgenre. More than one other work must be described by its category and preferably several, so where are they?

As a response to this lunatic theory, Stravinsky considers changing professions. The people he knows who claim to know something about the larger world insist peculiar new computer-things will soon be available for use by absolutely everyone especially including people without degrees from certified institutions of education, musical and otherwise. If he needs to know what the newest bandwagon to climb aboard is, he is promised this certainly is it!

Stravinsky prides himself on being the most up-to-date person he knows, so when he hears about these computer-things, he wonders if he has fallen a step or two behind; not far behind since he also knows composers of modern western classical music drifting much farther behind. But this device being described seems especially different; it is not a question of which toothpaste to choose or one's favorite style of shoe to wear, but instead what future music must eventually sound like. Stravinsky imagines a future whose issues and their contours are both opaque and terrifying and so unrecognizable. Every true future must be a location which tempts the rest of us to run toward, not flee from. If not, the danger is that the past will appear intriguing and even attractive, while the future lurks as a midnight dark terrain of fear and threat and doubt. How can such a future be a place to which the rest of us will eagerly turn?

Beavering away over many hours as he happily does, Arthur Honegger completes his most recent railroad locomotive symphony, and this one he titles "Consolidation 2-8-0".

Ives wonders whether any strategies remain which will reward his compositions with serious money plus also attract young women, or even just one. After all, aren't those the reasons composers of modern western classical music force themselves through corrosive hoops of training and practice to earn a degree that prepares them to crawl through even more hoops? Isn't all that what Ives assumes he must do in order to write good music in the first place? Concerning question thus posed, he is less certain than he wants to be. Having completed music school, he reminds himself to assume he now knows more than enough to compose music and does not need to know more. In music school he listens closely to many dreary explanations concerning musical notes, their operation and employment, along with numerous chords and the ways they are most regularly abused, plus a lot of other stuff whose fractured recollections leave him as embarrassed as confused. However, he also knows musicians who know far more about all this music stuff than he does and yet they earn far less money than he does. Thus has always been the way of music and appears it always will be.

Ives is forced to concede that in the end there has never been very much money in this music, and any aspirations otherwise have always been thrilling but perverted fantasies.

Being somewhat younger than Stravinsky, Ives is certain there is a deep purpose to the use of the musical salt shaker which, without his even thinking about it, highlights the correct choice and most effective distribution of those black marks. Such thinking is easily mistaken for magic which he would happily communicate with certain others for a sufficient amount of money. Only later can he recognize that all those little black marks provide a vehicle by which others will attempt to communicate with him. This notion of communication with its suggestion that someone believes they know something or recognize something of interest to Ives, and perhaps even appear useful to him, has never burdened him excessively and he leaves questions of that sort to Satie who is deeply attracted to every mysterious nonsense.

Ives recalls that over time a significant number of composers of music practice and write in various and varied eras, certain their compositions include subtle and profoundly important messages which, once deciphered, must benefit humanity. And uncomfortably, Ives admires those delusions which appear significant even while he sympathizes with their beleaguered spouses and members of their extended families. What draws his deepest sympathy are the burdens they must endure; how they need to believe the course of human existence depends on the decipherment of their subtly disguised messages which lay just beneath the surface of their otherwise superficial if not trivial music.

He regrets with embarrassment that all of the music he composes is only music which anyone and even everyone should either enjoy or ignore. After all, how can he communicate something which he does not recognize as a communication let alone understand? The fact is, Ives has a clear idea of how little he actually knows. That is, he is conscious of how little he is conscious of. Isn't that what is reflected back to him in every composition he pens? Just like the rest of us, despite his urgent desire to learn things without actually knowing that he knows them, he needs to know a thing before he can share that thing with others. As with most of us, he is satisfied he knows just enough even if only just enough, although later he needs to admit that the little he knows is not enough for almost every purpose he imagines. Simply put; how can something Ives does not know benefit someone who does not know that Ives does not know it? He recognizes this as an annoying conundrum, unless it is a paradox; either way, he has no idea how it resolves. Baffled within his confusion, Ives returns to thinking about Schoenberg.

Schoenberg completes his eighty-second glass trombone quartet and Ives is uncomfortably impressed by such slovenly numericity and its implied number-worship. He finds Schoenberg's glass trombone quartets surprisingly boring when they are not mind-numbing and considers all of this deep into his nights while yet convinced a resolution is available which he simply fails to recognize. Everyone, or so he is assured, is always communicating something, but no one is communicating everything. Or so he is also assured.

Meanwhile Shostakovich and Prokofiev argue for the better part of a month as if that exercise will get their old band with its old charts and old players back together again. Each fantasizes the way the rest of us do; that a particular splinter of history will repeat but with fresh conquests and new victories ready to be celebrated. What they and we fail to admit is that the past is never the future, except sometimes and only in very narrow ways. Everything that is part of the future is that which has not yet occurred even if that which has occurred resembles something that remains in the future. Besides, his still-imaginary band threatens to become one where each of the players expects to be paid and regularly.

Of course, if either of them finds something to pay this so-called band with, that will be useful. But from what they see and hear, paying one more gathering of half-talented and thoroughly antiquated degenerates (which accurately describes those they can find to sit in with their band) will require a source of capital whose origin remains a mystery without a solution.

It is around this time that Albert Roussel comes up with what he hopes to convince others is an ingenious plan.

Roussel's idea is to form a band made up of very smart monkeys; not just your average smart monkey but the very smartest to be found (the band will be called Monkeys Smarter Than You), and train them to sing together, albeit in monkey language, while playing various musical instruments or at least gesturing with peculiar devices mistaken for musical instruments. Although these monkeys never perform quite as well as humans who have completed music school, Roussel is certain that as long as the audience recognizes the tune, everyone will become millionaires. Except for the monkeys who, for obvious reasons, will never become millionaires. And if particular female members of the audience find these players less than charming, the explanation is that, like King Kong, these monkeys possess profound and musical souls which offer each a chance at personal redemption which itself remains the unifying element underlying the consciousness of all higher primates especially those who attempt to play music.

Upon hearing all of this, Ives simply shakes his head, reminding himself that if he believes half the things he is told, he must eventually become twice as stupid as he is. He then reminds himself how fortunate he is to remember hardly anything he is told and even less of what he sees. Simply put, the things he hears, like that which he sees, eventually abandon him and so open space within his brain for additional inconsequential things. In this way musical notes are liberated to dance before his eyes as tiny black fireflies in whatever way they wish and safe from being accosted by the rules of any composer including Ives.

Roussel hoards his ideas for musical compositions refusing to share them with anyone, especially anyone who can read music. As a teenager he is ruthlessly generous, offering what he does not have as what belongs to others and so accumulates favors certain that they will remain available when he needs them. But then Roussel asks Ives to review a composition offered by a student Rossel is unable to tolerate, Ives refuses and without batting an eye.

Ives insists to anyone who will listen that one becomes seriously confused and risks going blind scrutinizing student work and he has endured his very last headache in that struggle. He wants to explain all of this to Roussel while Roussel remains insufferably pompous and presumptuous. He behaves as if Ives' agreement is automatic, whereas Ives is even more annoyed with Roussel than he is with any of Roussel's inept students. And hasn't Stravinsky warned Ives that close scrutiny of student work rots the brain from within and returns nothing except a weak bladder and a flaccid pay-check?

So Charles Ives remains concerned by possible brain-rot which he does not deserve since he has always tried his best to be helpful or at least not hostile in a personal yet impersonal way.

Brecht assures Ives that this incantational paralysis is the sort of trap composers of modern western classical music risk; not hopeless but deeply discouraging. But if this is the end of something, for Ives it must be the end of something involving some other thing. Then comes Stravinsky bellowing a stream of bad words about Hindemith. Ives hopes that as the beacon of this terminal century fades there is another path of negotiation. He sees enough to decide such discord must all be Stravinsky's doing since his expanding collection of wives and mistresses demands an expanding income. Hindemith, meanwhile, remains busy counting all that money he is certain Disney will send him; he will keep all of it and damn anyone who thinks otherwise. This may be the worst element of composing modern western classical music; everyone with vaguely functioning ears is a critic. Despite tone-deafness, there is a perversion for every opinion.

Ives eventually suspects everyone is now composing modern western classical music since it is so easy to do. Plus also, ink and staff paper are now incredibly cheap. Despite often being dead, Milhaud writes more music than Beethoven ever threw away, a fact that the creepy perverts among the Back to Bach Movement even pretend to approve. As if to say; somebody must hit the jackpot writing modern western classical music, so why not me. Thus, he wonders if he will ever meet anyone who is not writing modern western classical music, and if so, will he recognize that person as human.

Ives considers going around the corner to Luciano Berio's Pizza Shop and then hesitates; he recalls that Berio has recently discovered that Ives fronts his own band (this new one he's calling Charley and The Silly Buggers). With that, every time Ives enters this pizza shop, along with whatever Ives orders, Berio shoves a stack of music manuscript across the counter asking that Ives tell him what he thinks. The thing is that, besides smears of red pizza sauce and a powdering of flour, Ives recognizes this guy must be left-handed since the musical notes are written backwards and face in the wrong direction; a sure sign of the musically self-taught. Ives grits his teeth having no patience for autodidacts, regardless of how skillful they insist they are. Besides, Ives fails to discover a reason to trust left-handed people. Being asked to review a composer's work as if something Ives owes to every pretend composer is an unfair imposition to burden Ives's as a composer of modern western music to his fury and lament.

Bartok, on the other hand, goes into Berio's Pizza and never has music manuscripts shoved at him. Ives considers letting Berio in on Bartok's secret. But with Ives' luck, Bartok will read that manuscript and then like it, following which he will attempt to promote it until there is a recording, which is then surprisingly well-received and results in Berio's composition finding startling popularity. On the other hand, if word gets out that Ives is offered this same composition and then decides to use its pages to line the bottom of his canary's cage, his reputation along with every potential of being paid plumets. What will he do for income after that?

Meanwhile, the popular even if occasionally dead Milhaud completes a new ballet/opera entitled, "Put It Where You Want It", concerning a boy interior-decorator and a girl interior-decorator who meet and fall in love and decide to marry but the client refuses, insisting their marriage will never match the drapes and rugs.

Ezra Pound, chief music critic for some major metropolitan newspaper, sits through this premier performance gritting his teeth, and at the end jumps from his seat and rushes to his newspaper's office where he writes a scathing review that ends with the assertion that modern western classical music is so utterly dead its odor can only be compared to that of fish. Completing this, he packs his bags and journeys to his ancestral castle in the mountains where he finds some gratification raising dental floss.

With all of this turmoil, little note is made of the premier of Auric's newest comic ballet/opera entitled, "Can't Beat Him With A Stick", in which a masochistic boy and a sadistic girl fall in love and decide to marry but the rug-shop owning dominatrix refuses to allow it with many comic moments and a peculiarly happy ending.

Meanwhile, now living at the far end of town, Stravinsky hires a contractor to install one of his several pianos at the bottom of one of his several swimming pools. Having taken up scuba diving he insists that piano music when played under water resonates with a shimmering, iridescent sound quality he has never even imagined and decides to record this marvelous sound. With the piano installed, his negotiations for the RCA recording contract eventually cost him a particularly succulent offer from Decca, yet he is certain that with this new recording technique, the world of modern western classical music will find itself flipped entirely onto its head. Finally.

Unsurprisingly and given the risk of disaster in mid-recording along with all the complications and unavoidable scandal leading to staggering court costs followed by an enormous insurance pay-out if such a disaster results, recording contact negotiations collapse; no one is prepared to sign him up, let alone promise any noticeable amount of money in exchange.

———————

Shostakovich and Prokofiev, returning from court after again trashing another hotel room, vehemently disagree with Stravinsky as well as each other over swimming pool music, and with such urgency that a tv interview program ends up in one more on-screen fistfight. The next day's newspapers feature humiliating photos of composers of modern classical music punching each other's faces and drawing blood. The moderator and her assistant stand to one side breathless with laughter, uncurious about whoever pays attention to Russian composers.

The ultimate challenge remains; if this is the best that modern western classical music can produce, has its form of composition and performance finally reached its limit? And if so, can the rest of us leave now?

Karl Heinz-Stockhausen's solution is to purchase twenty children's toy pianos and hire twenty children to play them. Gassed-up with bags of sugar treats, he unleashes them upon said pianos with the request they all play whatever they like and for as long as they can. He is convinced the minds of very young children are driven by impulses which must result in music of particular charm and grace. Besides, these kids work for jelly beans.

Following the release of Stockhausen's recording, these same children are hired by the Boston Pops Orchestra while Stockhausen is arrested for violations of the child labor laws. Many lawyers and months of court actions and large piles of money must clash and change hands before those charges are dismissed.

Bartok remains unintimidated. With the release of his trombonephone concerto entitled, "Twenty-Seven Uncomfortable Movements For Used Toilet-Plunger", he finds he is surprisingly hungry and passing Berio's Pizza Shop he is tempted to stop-in. But he decides against when he recalls what he's heard from Ives and so chooses McDonald's instead.

———————

By keeping his ear to the grape vine, Ives learns of the Daffy Duck Composer's Award competition being held by Warner's. Launched in response to the Minnie Mouse Achievement Award for Modern Western Classical Music Composition at Disney Studios, its composers must at least be old enough to know who Daffy Duck is. Such competitions—and Ives is grateful that each year there seems at least a few new ones—are among the remaining places where he has a moderate chance of making some money. And like every other composer of modern western classical music, he is relieved these awards are always paid in unmarked bills passed in unremarkable envelopes small enough to slip into a pants-pocket, along with an obnoxious bronze disc or plaque or, worse, some insulting modern sculpture (when did they stop using figures of charmingly naked women as such a prize?). Somewhat lucrative awards and contracts aside, there is little money available to composers of modern western classical music, and not nearly enough for Ives to earn a living. Yet, he is assured mounds of money lay about if, as a musician, he knows where to look and is quick enough at the snatch.

Still sniffing around for paying work, to his despair Ives discovers that Georges Auric is collaborating with Ferruccio Busoni to write a series of textbooks for students of advanced song-guessing: Vol. I; Why Did The Chicken Cross The Road? /What Do You Care?; Vol. II, Why Did The Chicken Cross The Road? /You're Asking Me?; Vol. III, Why Did The Chicken Cross The Road? /I Thought You Knew; and Vol. IV, Why Did The Chicken Cross The Road? /You And Who Else Wants To Know? A fifth and hopefully final volume of index, glossary and supplemental examples is now in preparation. The series is expected to aid advanced students of song-guessing at the collegiate level and that justifies its ridiculously high price.

Still wondering where he might pick up similar work, Ives learns that Alban Berg and Kurt Weill have snared the contract to write the music for the new cartoon movie titled, "Bugs Bunny Meets Mickey Mouse", the first in a projected series of Warners/Disney co-productions. In this first film, after a series of hilarious misadventures, Bugs Bunny shoots Mickey Mouse dead.

Understandably, Disney hates that ending, but then Walt sees the box-office returns he green-lights the sequel, "Bugs Bunny Meets Mickey Mouse Again", wherein it turns out that everything that happens in the first film is a dream.

Considering the money from particular contracts that drift by like ocean liners in the twilight, a serious composer of modern western classical music hesitates.

Deep in his music laboratory basement, Poulenc spreads fermata like fertilizer over his most recent septet for harmocarina, melophonium, intra-bassoon, and four other otherwise unspecified musical instruments which must not be any form of keyboard. Titled, "Land Mines For Lunatics" he originally composes it to accompany an epic film set during WW I and ti-tled, "Dance Of The First-Sergeants", in which a boy soldier and a girl soldier fall in love and plan to marry but their commander refuses his permission and so compels them to surrender to the enemy where they are permitted to marry and then live happily ever after to the frustration of their commander but delight of their audiences. For obvious reasons, the success of this film surprises the industry but also leads to a sound-track album which proves to be a holiday hit.

Once again returned from death, Stravinsky is furious to hear all of this since he convinces himself that actually it would have been his idea if he hadn't died first. Grinding his teeth but relieved that war-era music still makes money, he completes work on a new ballet/opera involving the WW II tank battle of Kursk and titled, "Tanks For The Mammarys", wherein a boy tank-commander and a girl tank-commander fall in love and announce their plan to marry but their divisional commander refuses his permission until Marshall Zhukov learns that the girl has fabulous breasts and immediately countermands the order resulting in cheers from everyone involved except the divisional commander. All of this is accompanied on stage by a chorus of twenty-four carefully trained braying wildebeests. Because it is a comedy, Stravinsky is certain of its success. His main concern is how to pay the drivers of twelve T-34 tanks which must rumble across the stage without crushing the cast, crew, wildebeests or the band.

Things for Ives are desperate. Each time he dies he returns to life poorer and also more annoyed. Recently he has spoken with his business manager who manages both Ives' income and his contracts asking where the money has gone with which occasionally he is paid.

His business manager, T. S. Elliot, shrugs confessing he has no idea where Ives' money might be but he has not seen any of it. Speaking as his business manager he reminds Ives that if he really wants money, he should put out a 'Greatest Hits' recording to capture a slice of all that delirious holiday overspending which every other composer of modern western classical music must chase on hands and knees. Ives asks what any Greatest Hits album has to do with his still-missing money which is missing because Elliott fails to keep track of it. To which Elliot then snorts and sniffs, whining that if the money wasn't missing, there would be no need to call it missing money, now would there? He then reminds Ives that, in any case, Stravinsky is working on his own Greatest Hits album and does Ives assume Stravinsky is stupidly wasting his time?

Ives is even more annoyed than surprised when Elliot claims that all Ives needs to do to acquire new money is put more black marks on white paper after which checks will appear regularly and with very large numbers written on them. Whereas poor suffering Elliot is compelled to do actual work for his money while tolerating insults and abuse from one more incompetent and ungrateful composer who insists Elliot is at fault anytime even the littlest bit of money becomes misplaced. His only fault is that all he ever wants to do is lay in a hammock strung between two trees in his underwear in his backyard and read pornography. He then reminds Ives that Dylan Thomas still does that and for money and nobody gives him grief. In fact, he's paid even more money than most musicians including the mildly successful ones, unlike failures like Ives.

He then bursts into tears insisting in his most pathetic voice that he, being Elliot, is doing the best he can and all of this is so totally unfair and anyway why isn't Ives dead again unless he is already dead and fails to notice since he is otherwise such an abject musical failure. Ives concludes there will be no new answers to whatever has happened to his money.

Ives then wonders if he should hire a new manager but one who keeps track of his money and also finds his other money, plus also finds a few paying jobs for him and his new band (this one he calls Charlie and the Masters of the Broken Wind). He hears that Stravinsky has hired a particularly good business manager named Auden who only steals small amounts of money occasionally and still keeps Stravinsky's bookings loaded up so that he works and gets paid right to the end of the year. A frustrated Ives refuses to be surprised.

Poulenc, meanwhile, is at it again and expects everyone to notice. His most recent coup comes when Republic Pictures picks up his contract from M-G-M and assigns him to compose the score for their newest bio-pic, a film titled, "Can You Hear Me Now?' that tells the true story of a young Alexander Graham Bell walking the length and breadth of the country planting telephone pole seeds as he goes, and then returns in the fall when they have grown as telephone poles ripe for being strung with telephone lines. People then discover it is much easier to lie to each other and over longer distances especially in time for the holidays when people need to lie about those gifts they are never going to send.

Poulenc hates this project since he seriously hates telephones since they never provide him any good news except when informing him of the death of one of the many impoverished modern western classical music enemies. Yet he finds it impossible to refuse this job when his business manager, Octavio Paz, who teaches himself English just so he can get in in the midst of all these piles of musician's money, reminds Poulenc he still owes payments on his Triumph motorcycle, as well as alimony payments for his three most recent wives. He regrets having to remind Poulenc of his numerous child-support payments for his offspring, the unsurprising result of his being a randy composer of modern western classical music. Usually, it demands a lot to embarrass Poulenc, but Paz's litany pretty well does that job. He then asks Paz how much music Republic Pictures actually expects him to deliver. When Paz informs him approximately three hours (it is for a bio-pic, after all), Poulenc laughs until his face turns red after which he checks himself into a well-respected and very expensive rehabilitation clinic.

Unfortunately, shooting on the Bell film has already begun and the two other films expecting to be accompanied by Poulenc's music have nearly complete scripts, so executives at Republic, hearing this response along with the astronomical costs of Poulenc's rehab, discuss tossing themselves from the tops of their very high office buildings on the chance that will solve their problem or they will learn to fly.

But when Ives puts himself forward to cover whatever music Poulenc fails to produce, the chiefs at Republic simply laugh and laugh; a gesture they are highly skilled at when dealing with composers of modern western classical music

---

Schoenberg watches all of this with growing consternation. He attempts to hire Elliot away from Ives suspecting that Elliott may be the best candidate to run his thoroughly corrupt non-profit constructed to funnel the money he must hide from drummers and other percussionists as well as ex-spouses into a secure and highly secret bank account.

Following his most recent death, Schoenberg considers a career change. Hearing the music Debussy composes for one more manufacturer of large and ugly cars he is certain the music to promote such cars must be at least as shapely as the obnoxious machines it promotes. He then finds himself captured by a paranoid vision of his status within the pantheon of composers of modern western classical music pathetically engaged in cranking out tunes to advertise mechanical vehicles, and he trembles at what he fears he sees.

Ravel, on the other hand, simply chuckles, grateful that the harder he squeezes these suckers, the more money comes out.

Alban Berg on the other hand finds he has reached a limit. His cash reserve trails along at some remarkably low level. Fortunately, he has paid his back-dues to the musician's union and so believes he is back in the good graces of its shop steward, who this year is Leonard Bernstein, elected on the promise to his membership that there will be paying work for every musician who wants it, including those writing and performing modern western classical music.

Berg looks about the union hall relieved he already knows this is a pile of crap and he is as unlikely to work now as he ever has been; as if it is ever the case that money must follow work. Besides, along with unpaid alimony payments, he is attempting to ignore certain car payments. One can find work without a spouse, but it is impossible to find work without a car, and worse, ever find a spouse without work and a car—it all dovetails together, sort of.

Unfortunately, the finance company shows no interest in repossessing any of his ill-conceived marriages—and why might they wish to—yet that same finance company eagerly makes his car disappear and legally. Berg knows he must drop a few payments on them while they're still watching, if only for old-time sake and as a way of his saying hello, I'm still here and still need this damn crappy car.

Berg wonders what Schoenberg's next project will amount to, and several other composers wonder the same. But since he has no way of knowing without asking, and also because the weather remains exceptionally pleasant, Berg decides it is the right day to go to the rat races, where he hasn't lost money in more than a week. Regularly losing money betting the rat races, he knows this must change soon because nothing can go on forever, unless it does.

Besides, little stirs Berg's composer's blood or generates desperate and frantic new ideas like the squeals and aromas of sleekly-muscled racing rats and their dung.

For logical and psychological reasons, Berg stands close to the rats' racing cages even though that guarantees the dogs chasing those rats around the course with their baying and howling and snarling and other rat-terrifying sounds must pass directly behind him. Happily, Berg has only been bitten by the chase-dogs two or three times while his trousers are torn rather often. He knows those dogs intend him no personal harm; they are just as excited to be chasing these rats as Berg is to watch.

Berg is certain he is due for a break; something must snap his string of loses and all the money those loses have cost. This cannot be simple bad luck. Berg remembers a story, certainly a cautionary tale, involving Albert Rossel and his band from several years back, The Rusty Hex-Nuts (a deeply cheesy sorcery band with black masks and spooky music), and the most recent time he has fronted a band.

The way Berg hears Roussel's tale—and he knows there are several versions—Roussel leads his eighteen-piece catastrophe which features an all-hits repertoire of popular tunes played in the style of modern western classical music. Despite this, unless it is because of this, the band enjoys substantial bookings. As best as Roussel can figure, these bookings should continue through the approaching holidays. Since their paychecks drop like clock-work (at least like clock-work for a musician), Roussel pays his band once a week rather than after each performance. But one week, instead of paying his band, since he is certain there will be another paycheck after this one, he takes the band's pay to the rat races. After all, he cannot keep losing forever, he knows these rats and their reputations too well. The only question is how much money he will win.

At the rat races Roussel stands close to the racing cages, certain the racing rats recognize his words of encouragement. On this afternoon he is so confident he bets the entire packet of the band's pay reminding himself that he is not greedy but simply enjoys possessing money more than most composers of modern western classical music.

And as so often happens in his real life as opposed to his optimistic imaginary life, all of Roussel's rats finish out of the money. He finds he must now think of who he hasn't borrowed money from. He considers for a moment returning to selling drugs, but since every other composer supplements his income likewise, it is instantly obvious he can never earn enough to pay the band. But he must admit his musicians are not artists with alternate sources of income and so might wait patiently to be paid. With his problems layering over each other yet all involving money, Roussel sells the copywrite to all of the music he has written up to this moment and to a person who has become famous by scribbling feeble and often annoying lyrics to music that resembles trick-and-roll music. Exercises in that regard conjure a lot more money than either Roussel himself or anyone he knows. Having settled for a pittance sufficient to his need as his price of copywrite, Roussel finds that amount of money regrettably trivial.

When word of all this gets around, Roussel is embarrassed. As hard as it is for him to believe, he recognizes himself merely one more composer of modern western classical music furious over the amounts of money regularly paid to performers of that musical disaster labeled trick-and-roll. Utterly broke, no one is surprised when he returns to rough-frame carpentry.

———————

Brecht then hears that Stravinsky, following the installation of a piano at the bottom of one of his swimming pools and using scuba equipment, plans to record a series of performances of his greatest hits. Stravinsky insists to anyone who will listen, that a piano performance of his music underwater must sound compelling and thrilling and so demands the re-release of all his old work. These new recordings, he claims, will provide unexpected avenues for music appreciation while earning him additional money from work previously done; like being paid twice for the same kiss.

And then one evening, Honegger is sitting at the bar at the Club Paradise Canceled and on the band's break one of the glass trombone players Honegger believes is named Jake sits down on the stool beside him and after complaining the club owner expects the band's members pay for their own beers asks Honegger if he's heard anything about some sort of music festival held someplace not nearby. Honegger shrugs because he hasn't and then the glass trombone player nods saying he thought so since nobody he's talked to has heard about it either and then stands chuckling with the comment that this is where he came in.

As the band then kicks off the next set, Honegger wonders what such a festival might look like, but even more, what such a festival might sound like, and how much money could be made. As the band plays, Honegger wonders.

––––––––––

Finally bored with his current motorcycle, a possession he dreamed about as a child of twenty-three or twenty-four, Satie discovers that somehow it has outlived its fantasy. It is unsurprising that ten years needs to pass for such a deep thrill to fade, but eventually his mind drifts about in search of a new yet thoroughly improved fantasy. He is relieved to find that his motorcycle distracts others from noticing his obvious limitations, particularly his peculiar body-odor, a challenge that has confronted music composers of every era, since in the midst of a compositional delirium, one rarely thinks to shower. He hopes that what others assume they recognize is the pungent aroma of vintage high-test gasoline and so disguise himself as one of the hapless composers of modern western classical music; sniveling, pathetic, anti-social, unmarriageable and broke. Unfortunately, as useful as such a perception might once have been, it is obviously useless today. And so he wonders if finally motorcycles as a broad category of overpriced and redundant but extremely noisy fantasies, has exhausted its acceptance.

Ives wrestles with one more baffling writer's block and in search of a cure wanders into the Sixteenth Note Bar & Grill where Poulenc's new band, The Huffing Puffers, are doing a miserable job determined to slaughter Poulenc's newest composition, "High On Life" and thus render every fantasy of material income moot if not impossible. At the break he corners Poulenc and there offers his version of the rumor he's heard concerning some sort of music festival. Taller than Ives, Poulenc looks down wide-eyed and then burst into chilling laughter; he assures Ives that such a project is as likely to succeed as an attempt to harness snakes to a chariot. Unsure of exactly what he's been told, Ives reminds himself that Poulenc has gone to college.

––––––––––

Satie's current motorcycle still brings to mind those sweltering nights of careening across the countryside half-drunk on modern western classical music along with several grams of something else, yet no longer yields the thrill, the acidic forgetfulness or even the hysteria, of his youth. At his desk with pen in hand and black dots swimming before his eyes, he recalls the innocent thrill of riding out with Stravinsky and Prokofiev and Roussel, the self-designated Four Musiceteers straddling their roaring machines drunk as popes and determined to rip the peace from the night, abrading and searing its darkness, their futures those dreams which must become real. As if those futures could ever be less than a cascading sequence of blinding fireworks of acclaim. Memories drift before Satie's eyes and he just resists asking the question no one should ever ask, even in the most bitter night; whatever happened?

When did his future become his past? How did that which was limitless shrivel into this moment? He shakes his head and rubs his eyes promising himself a serious drunk, a compulsive and continual consumption of alcohol; the only therapy that will compel those hysterical black dots to calm down and find their way to their proper location on this clean white sheet of paper.

Less disciplined than moths, even more irritating than fleas, vulnerable to the slightest twitch or gentlest movement of air, those pesky black notes hop and/or fly and/or flee when they don't simply drift about undecided whether to land on different lines or different pages or just drift away altogether. And what else is modern western classical music except the sound of that very future coded as little black dots delivered fresh every morning to overlay another past. If Satie recognizes one thing, it is that the past is not the future except in an odd and unpleasant way. But if the future is merely the past in disguise, whatever can be the point of wondering?

Ives finds himself indifferent to any of this. The accumulation of disappointments assures him of what he must not expect. Baffled as always by that which he can see and yet fail to understand, he wonders half-aloud what music will sound like in that future when modern western classical music stops being modern in order to sound old-fashioned. He assumes that music will sound a particular way when played on yet-to-be-imagined musical instruments, if that future music still depends on sounding through a mechanical device, or instead arrives directly in the brains of an otherwise brain-dead audience compelled to gather experiences absent of any perceptible recognition or arbitrated context. He tries to imagine how that will sound, and whether audiences hearing some ditty written for example by Stravinsky but now played at a junior prom on a collection of impossible-to-imagine instruments will laugh with embarrassment. After which he wonders if, even out of curiosity, he should write a piece of music about writing a new piece of music which attempts to encapsulate the experience of writing a new piece of music whose subject is what it is that new music must sound like? Ives wonders whether, if he understands well enough, he will write a piece of music about that which he doesn't entirely understand or even understands at all. As if all of that did not describe a universe of its own and bound within the mind of Charles Ives.

Undaunted by anything that daunts other composers of modern western classical music, Honegger completes a surprisingly expansive and aggressive new railroad locomotive symphony, this one entitled "Berkshire 2-8-4".

––––––––

Milhaud spends the better part of his morning determined to get a particular cow off one of his roofs. He notices this cow through the kitchen window while preparing coffee. At first, he fails to wonder how this or any cow could get up there. The appearance of this cow must result in serious embarrassment in the eyes of his neighbors; roofs, he is prepared to concede, are not conventionally homes for cows. And worse, he knows that all of this cow-moving will cost him a bundle. Besides this, it is unlikely he will get any music composing done until he gets this stupid cow off of his stupid roof. As a cow, it is mostly white with large patches of brown and black appearing just as likely to have been painted onto it by someone resembling Bela Bartok. It does not appear a particularly hostile cow although Milhaud assumes its discontent at finding itself where it finds itself, and so he is certain their relationship will remain superficial even if this cow's occupancy of his roof is mistaken for affection, or something worse.

He recalls several cows in his past whose relationships were never deep nor long lasting, thereby justifying the fact that their names have disappeared from his memory. He insists that his relationship with this cow will not be any different from those others. But still, there is this cow on his roof and it stares longingly toward the ground while appearing with only a slight danger it will jump. So Milhaud wonders if this is one more of those days on which one learns to embrace affliction, even including from a cow unfortunately resident on one's roof.

For a moment he is tempted to compose something that celebrates this certainly temporary relationship, raising an intriguing question; how does one best document a relationship with a cow of unknown origin and uncertain temperament and for only a brief length of time? He considers a memorial in the form of music and named after this stupid cow; something like, "Stupid Cow Somehow On My Roof". He then wonders if this cow has a name or whether it wants one, but most especially whether it is at all tempted to go home. But even without knowing this cow's name, he must get it off of his roof. Inducements to depart, even the composition of a piece of music named after it, he recognizes as a badly-formed failure. Thus, Milhaud must acknowledge the fact that this is about to become complicated and also cost him more money than he prefers. The true cost of a cow on one's roof may be measureless even if not infinite.

———————

Stravinsky stands on the sidewalk across the street from Milhaud's cow-burdened bungalow and watches these ridiculous exercises with his arms folded, and he just laughs and laughs and laughs loudly enough for Milhaud to hear. Embarrassed neighbors standing nearby begin to move away as he continues to laugh. Being a composer of modern western classical music, irony with an addiction to discomforting others remain basic to Stravinsky's tool-box. Convinced not only that Milhaud knows nothing useful about the composition of modern western classical music, but that he knows even less about how to turn a baffling and embarrassing occasion like the discovery of a cow on one's roof, into a piece of music which a non-deaf person might pay money to hear.

And yet Stravinsky discovers involuntary admiration of Milhaud's dilemma. As he thinks of it, he sees other composers of modern western classical music standing about also mesmerized by the sight of this cow now rising with a crane from the roof of this unremarkable suburban home; a roof which in no way suggests it needs its own cow regardless of gender, size or color, positioned unstrategically and therefore blatantly on its roof. Annoyed by his confusion, Stravinsky scratches his head. He wonders if this is Milhaud's attempt to divert attention from the piano installed at the bottom of Stravinsky's swimming pool. Vaguely impressed by Milhaud's strategy, Stravinsky wonders about Ives and his college roommate, Stevens; is this all in anticipation of a performance likely to leave Stravinsky annoyed and with fewer fans? Or perhaps composers are so bemused by cows on roofs, they are incapable of accomplishing anything more than nothing. He is relieved to be unconcerned and is instead thoroughly bored.

Suddenly something flashes through Stravinsky's mind and he hurries back to his home. Quickly he completes the score as well as lyrics for an entirely new ballet/opera entitled, "Trading Zeitgeists For Weltanschauungs." But just to be certain this composition eclipses the attention drawn by Milhaud's cow, and with the debonaire panache of an impresario, he manages to convince the great mezzo-soprano, Phoebe Zeit-Geist herself, to come out of her retirement and sing the lead. Needless to say, every other composer of modern western classical music is furious with jealousy and a few even search out lawyers, as if such creatures could help a composer of modern western classical music.

Stravinsky's younger brother Gary (his birth name is Yuri, but that's a separate story- he always hated his name since it sounded so Russian) convinced that his older brother's profession can only be a money-farm, or at least a money bush, begins to compose modern western classical music that resembles Beethoven's. Gary's defense is that since Beethoven made so much money from his music, why shouldn't he. But the reaction of other composers so infuriates him that he decides to form his own trick-and-roll band where his musicians will play his music in a way that resembles Beethoven's but in a highly self-conscious and annoyingly modern style (and grateful there are no living heirs to Beethoven to contest the copywrite). Ives knows how hopeless this strategy will prove since it's been done so often before; he hears no mistresses or swimming pools in Gary's future.

And yet having himself an older brother who annoys him with every breath and possesses no future beyond his pathetic past, Ives feels sympathy for Gary. Ives even admits that Gary's most recent composition, "March of the Psychonauts," a concerto grosso featuring as soloists a melophonium and a tenor glass trombone, proves to be remarkably toe-tapping and nearly catchy. Still unconvinced of any likelihood Gary will earn serious money with this composition, Ives concedes it is an amiable effort and so is surprised when Igor has nothing to say about the composition or the brother who writes it.

With his cow finally off his roof and being no longer dead gives Milhaud several new ideas which he suspects may yield profitable compositions in the modern western classical music vein. Lately he has though a lot about soup operas along with their companion soup symphonies and the possibilities such compositions possess to earn serious money. He considers beginning work on a soup symphony entitled, "The Pinafore of Death", where the boy's part is played by a bazookoboe and the girl's part is played by an air-piccolotuba (unlike the harmocarina, it is an instrument Milhaud particularly favors although he never plays it well). The story involves a priest and a nun who fall in love but then realize they hate each other and so kill each other in the end. Due to all the bloodshed, this soup symphony proves exceptionally successful with audiences of small children who still, despite everything, love violence and the sight of blood.

––––––––––

Struggling with a burst of insupportable optimism, Ives once again attempts to put a band together (to be called Chuck and The Lip-Smacking Dollies), but this one skilled at wood-frame carpentry since he concludes that the only way to be certain to make money at this music thing is occasionally to stop making music altogether since the making of such music is a trap for not making any money at all. Being dead is when he and most musicians make the most money (audiences are regularly mistaken that dead composers of modern western classical music will write no more music, and so what has been written is all that ever will be recorded and released). Not being dead, Ives and his new band should make money, but they'll make even more money framing out split-level homes which beats attempting to teach teenagers to play the piccolotuba, or even how to hold that instrument properly.

Following their most recent arrest for trashing their hotel room, the partnership between Prokofiev and Shostakovich reaches a crisis from which neither is ready to back down. Both in love with Gertrud Stein (who herself confesses a lust for E. E. Cummings, whose heart has gone to Ginger Rogers), these annoying Russian composers refuse to concede and so drive their nearly non-existent fans into foggy-minded despair that ruins appetites and destroys sleep.

Despite tidal waves of pointless agitation and useless optimism, Rousel, having sold the copyrights to all of his composed music, considers taking up hydroponic farming, a profession that composers of modern western classical music are surprisingly well-adapted to undertake.

But as usual, Satie has other ideas and none of them about to make anyone happy or even make anyone any money although at least they have nothing to do with hydroponic farming.

Satie works for some time on a series of short compositions he gathers under the title, "Adventures of the Formerly-Buried", scored for eight alto harmocarinas and ten bubble-wrap percussionists. This follows his composition for combined and altered percussion entitled, "An Abundance of Malets", scored for an unspecified number of varying size drums but less than ten and with the entire ensemble tuned to the Dorian mode, one which Satie has heard recently and decides to take out on a date and discover if this mode puts out, like the Lydian.

Yet Satie recognizes that these are minor works more likely to be ignored than praised and certainly incapable of attracting money. Learning of Stravinsky's underwater piano, Satie decides he needs a gimmick of his own, something to attract attention without costing anything. But then he recalls that Ravel and Debussy manage to have careers without gimmicks unless their gimmick is to appear to not have any gimmick; a non-gimmick as a true gimmick, unless Satie has confused himself which is frequently the case.

But none of this sorts out Satie's complications or points in a direction along which he should proceed. He remembers Auric speaking to him about all of this. He no longer remembers what is said but Satie remembers stepping away from their conversation more annoyed then relieved. What might prove useful are song titles which sound so clever they pierce the mind in a helpless assault. With clever titles, the music behind them might attract the attention they deserve. What he discovers each time he peers through his musical microscope assures him that the music most musicians take for granted is devious and insincere and even self-mocking but certainly self-deceptive and as self-absorbed as any of their composers.

Ives is baffled as well as broke and remembers that story of Franz Joseph Haydn and his exorcism. According to what Ives might remember, once near midway through his fourth novel (later to be published under the title, "Pay No Attention To The Man Behind The Bathroom Door", wherein a detective investigates the strange sounds and repulsive odors escaping from behind a bathroom door), Haydn finds himself burdened by a particularly irritating writer's block and decides his only hope for moving his novel forward is exorcism. This strategy fails to tempt Ives and he wonders if there is some other way to tap into some hidden cache of ideas he has forgotten. As everyone agrees, Haydn's novel emerges a massive hit and spawns two tv series; so much money changes hands for so little work that composers of modern western classical music simply shake their heads and sigh.

Resigned that theft is no bad idea, Ives lifts Roussel's name for a former band and begins work on what turns out to be his most successful ballet/opera, "The Hex-Nuts Go To College", which tells the story of a boy-Satanist and a girl-Satanist attending university who decide to go to law school but then following their emergency exorcism they change their minds and decide to pursue vegetarian philosophy; a most anguishing and bloody tragedy whose darkness is enhanced by even more darkness. The public reception for this work startles even Ives' business manager who unfortunately remains T. S. Elliott, and who immediately cashes the resulting check at the rat-races to which he has been addicted, much to Ives' impoverishment. Far worse, still needing money he must sell the performance rights for "Hex-Nuts" to Alban Berg, recently no longer dead and looking to put together a new band of his own. Berg searches for a new book of arrangements plus a new business manager and booking agent who is not a former let alone currently practicing Satanist. That person must also have avoided prison since Berg already has problems which involve Satan and his Satanists (Anton Weber's newest band), which shows a bit of traction among the sixty-year-old to eighty-years-old crowd.

Satanists, former, current or future, make the most effective business managers; their skills at negotiating contracts recognized as unearthly. Once

Ives finds the right business manager, he is certain the cash will arrive in buckets. And Ives knows exactly what he will do with those buckets of money.

Stravinsky, possessor of numerous buckets of money, frets over those buckets of money he does not possess and his current business manager is no longer eager to retrieve for him. It appears he must re-enter that marketplace for something resembling a business manager. All the while, no-talents like T. S. Elliot puff themselves to the music community over their superior competence and so call themselves business managers instead of occupants of unhealthy and unprofitable prison cells. If Stravinsky ever forgives Elliott for all of the buckets of money he has misplaced, that exercise in humiliation will need to take place in some other dimension.

Relieved that he is no longer dead, Milhaud asks about royalty checks arriving while he is dead and so deposited in his checking account but which he has yet to locate. Of course, his first thought is that T. S. Elliot has struck again but Shostakovich assures him that Elliott has recently been behind bars for emptying the bank account of Prokofiev. At Elliott's trial he is embarrassed to admit he simply hasn't had the time to empty each bank account he has access to. Besides, Milhaud has so little money that Elliott fails to find its temptation interesting. But Milhaud's first thought is to call Georges Auric, who he recalls speaks Spanish, plus also knows that Picasso owes Milhaud money.

Bartok remains a busy drunk composer of modern western classical music as an icon of modern art; what more could he want? At the small, round table in the motel room he rents desperate to get relief from his wife and their eleven children, as well as his nasty-mouthed mother-in-law, he works to complete his most recent composition, "Machines In Absentia", the score for a film based on a script written by Blaise Cendras with additional dialogue by Max Jacob about a girl-machine who falls in love with a boy-machine and they decide to marry but their robot minister refuses to allow it since the boy-machine is A/C and the girl-machine is D/C. Hopeful of union support, Bartok scores the piece for a choir of glass trombones since that sound conveys the most humor while tinged with a sort of depraved anguish. This motel room, like his work on this composition, remains boring and so demands more discipline since it leaves him that much more vulnerable to drink and its delightful distractions.

Determined to never again put all of his eggs into a single musical basket regardless of how musical it appears, Bartok negotiates with Marcel Duchamp hopeful that he will shake out of him a reference for a job at the natural gas plant. Bartok decides he should plan to never be paid enough money to pay for all of the braces and other dental devices his eleven children will need, never mind the cost of sending even one of them to college.

Duchamp warns Bartok that none of this is likely but Bartok remains optimistic about a contract with M-G-M, one more assumption that must lead to brutal disappointment. Unhappily for Bartok, optimism continues to cost him much and nearly every day.

Since he pays no attention to any of this and so is able to write even more music, Honegger completes still one more railroad locomotive symphony which he entitles with a smile, "Union Pacific Big Boy 4-8-8-4".

Wallace Stevens hears that Ives has returned from wherever he was and with a new ballet/opera in hand titled, "Pull The Other One", a contemporary romp involving a boy stand-up comedian and a girl stand-up comedian who fall in love and decide to marry except the manager of the comedy club refuses permission certain their marriage will not be very funny. Stevens hates this ballet/opera even more than he hates all of the previous ones, yet he admires Ives' tenacity and determination even if his attempt at this sort of comedy makes Stevens squirm, especially this ballet/opera's finale involving children of various ages recruited from a near-by orphanage and dressed as comedians. Stevens guesses how broke Ives must finally be and so how desperate he is. He only wonders if it is time to have that talk with Stravinsky; there must be some way to stop this bold-faced musical pilferage, a conscienceless but effective brigandage.

Stevens confesses, at least to himself, that these purported musicians as composers of modern western classical music are more annoying than baffling. Why expect to be paid simply for making black dots on sheets of otherwise innocent white paper; this question confuses him but also annoys him. If this only involves numbers, he can imagine at least a justification for the interest and even enthusiasm for this poorly-packaged cacophony. But none of that makes sufficient sense, and not making sense makes it that much more annoying and so the last thing Stevens finds tolerable. He spends hours determined to convince Ives the future is not the past, and so if he hopes to be paid significant money, he must concentrate his efforts on something not yet in the past regardless of how badly it smells.

But Stevens also knows that Ives possesses nearly-infinite patience for the most boring activities. Otherwise, how could he tolerate the composing of modern western classical music? With a smile he recalls those months Ives spent working as a roofer under a frying sun or slapped by freezing wind while perched on various roofs breathing in noxious vapors; composing modern western classical music might be even more physically damaging as well as more frightening than roofing.

————

Shostakovich beavers away at another quartet for piccolotuba, tenor and bass glass trombones and harmocarina while also working on a separate composition whose title, at least for the moment, is "Arms Akimbo", a ballet/opera involving thirty-eight singing belly dancers and an harmocarina chorus of approximately seven to forty-three performers depending on the cost of two weeks of rehearsals. As is usual for a composer of modern western classical music, he refuses to confess that this piece originates from an idea stollen from Satie which some suspect is originally stolen from Ferdinand Leger. In a subsequent interview. Leger insists he remains contemptuous of all forms of music, musicians and their scabby and foul-smelling compositions. Further, he suggests Shostakovich stole the original idea from Carlos, the delivery kid from Berio's Pizza Palace; one more secret and baffled composer of modern western classical music.

Not that any of this is ever admitted by anyone, including Carlos who remains royally pissed-off about this rip-off and for nearly half a minute considers calling a lawyer.

Determined not to be outdone, Prokofiev rushes to complete his own quartet for glass trombones entitled, "Clowns At The Beach", its score is complete through the first three movements. Its story involves three clowns, two male and one female, who become furious when their clown-make-up gets covered in sand which is painful to wipe off and so argue as to whose bright idea it is to go to the beach. What is instantly obvious to anyone with ears is that only so many musicians are sufficiently skilled with their instruments, especially when it comes to performing modern western classical music.

Shostakovich wonders, given the cost of hiring skilled players, whether his past would have been better-spent becoming an accomplished player himself and at least assure himself a steady income. Then he recalls Prokofiev and his quartet of piccolotuba players and that they remain an odorous group which Shostakovich still finds annoying if not offensive. He can't decide whether there is even a splinter of musical thought produced by Prokofiev unless the question involves instrumentation. Shostakovich questions his own work while considering Ives and the silly stuff he pumps out mistakenly confident someone will put money beside it. What finally annoys him is that Ives is determined to compose the least offensive music of any modern western classical music composer, undoubtedly a doomed strategy anyone can only find offensive. Unless it earns money.

––––––––––

Roussel insists that Auric apologize for all the appoggiaturas he is using, having already used so many there seem hardly any left for anyone else. Cadential perversions is how Roussel labels it with a sneer; if only Dallapiccola was not dead again, this would not be a problem. He seems to have a restraining influence on Auric even if no one knows exactly how or why.

With all of this in mind, Roussel begins a new ballet/opera he titles, "A Nod To A Blind Horse", wherein a boy horse and a girl horse discover they like each other and do horse-type things until one day a storm approaches and they agree to wait it out under a tall and broad tree where a lightning bolt suddenly strikes splitting the tree's trunk to the ground and the horses are electrocuted and so die together within sight of each other and at the very same moment; Roussel is certain there will be sniffles and tears all the way to the concession stand.

Hearing all of this through waves of nauseating sentimentality, Auric insists that for his next composition he will write a passacaglia consisting of a nearly endless stream of unresolved triple appoggiaturas which he will title, "Stranger Here Than Elsewhere"; the story of a boy astronaut and a girl astronaut who fall in love are thwarted by all of the strange things that go on around them. To Auric's relief, more than one orchestra shows interest in performing its premier, providing a bidding war which should hand him a gold mine even if a tiny one, plus also assure that his next composition will earn him somewhat more than the last. With all of this in place, Auric turns to the design of the t-shirt with a boost from Miro.

Seeing all this, Blaise Cendrars recognizes the idiocy of Auric's strategy, insisting that once you have the right design for the t-shirt, the music and its accompanying royalty checks must surely follow. With this in mind, he invites Marc Chagall to help design a t-shirt that will image the thematic profligacy of this newest composition, a bouquet albeit brief and unembarrassed, of cadential progressions and their pseudo-anonymous inversions; its title can only be, "Doctor Porkenstein and The Chamber of Mysterious Sandwiches", a relentless tale of murder, mayhem and mustard followed by death, lots and lots of death. RCA shows interest.

But scrutiny by the restless, distracted and bored masses is itself relentless and Chagall is certain that if he argues against this plan, pianists like Nicolai Mayakovski will simply make fun of him and remind him that in fact two wrongs simply make a third wrong for which no one will be grateful, plus also his royalty check will be that much smaller.

––––––––––

Ives follows these developments from a distance and with a skeptical eye certain that behind all of this lay something else which may also be a lie but then again maybe it isn't. He scratches his head thinking of Debussy.

Sometimes Ives does not think at all about Debussy and recognizes those as among the happier days, unburdened by thoughts of France or anyone who speaks French. But those days are not these days and Ives assumes that if those days ever return, it won't be very soon. So what, in the meantime, should he do?

Like most composers of modern western classical music, Ives is proud to the point of vanity of composing very convincing elephant calls and cow moos. Whereas Stravinsky is proud to the point of arrogance about his success at conjuring the music of a yard-full of chickens, as if that is remarkable. Since every animal produces particular sounds, the range and selection of certain sounds far exceed the distinctions among musicians themselves. But audiences have become jaded with that subtle darkness of the trombonophone from which profound and sultry but also syrupy sounds arise, as if just any fake magic could hold sway over an easily-distracted audience for modern western classical music.

With all this, Ives begins work on a new composition which he does by slinging a platter of appoggiaturas against the wall (he prefers his kitchen's wall to his bathroom) and then transcribing what sticks. In preparation for this he reviews exercises involving atonal counterpoint even though Ives is aware, just as nearly every other composer of modern western classical music is, that current forms of counterpoint are overdone and to death. But Ives and nearly every other composer of modern western classical music is also certain that the moment audiences remember to miss it, counterpoint, atonal or otherwise, will return. So why, he asks himself as if he is someone else and there is no one else to ask, spend more time wasting time? The question strikes him like a latent cadenza, all grey and smelling of long-dead fish.

That question at the center of his thoughts, he begins a work which must strike at the soul of his generation, "Talking To Machines", a tale of a boy-computer and a girl computer who discover their programs match so intimately that their manufacturer must blow them to smithereens to prevent them from reproducing and thus taking over the planet and destroying all human beings except for shapely teenagers dancing at the beach who have deciphered their computer dialect. Accompanied by a chorus of twenty ninth-grade children supported by an orchestra of percussion and non-percussion instruments, Ives once again worries over where the money for rehearsals will come from.

Certain rhythmic motifs dominate the universe of modern western classical music and for far too long, unless not quite long enough. He is reminded that compositions which involve the intrabasson demand cascades of tremolos and glissandi in order to conjure a peculiar sound described in a German word which Ives cannot pronounce but translates as 'ear-fart'; that is, a patch of music that smells worse than it sounds.

In the course of his search for discarded or previously used latent cadenzas, Ives stumbles onto several lose canons in contrary motion. He admits they resemble something he does not recognize but stirs a sudden urgency to compose a piece involving quarter-tone rows in the form of a sforzando to end with a rondo ritmico. Less delighted than confused, he is at least mildly relieved. And he avoids just barely a descent into dodecaphonism; a skin irritation of the hands and lower arms that plages many composers of modern western classical music when they are not dead. Stravinsky, as usual, is scathing in his dismissal of certain musical mechanics although complete silence remains more challenging than noisy indifference.

Just then, Milhaud completes a series of seven bitonal bagatelles he titles, "Death For Beginners", before he contacts Disney, confident it is the type of project they will instantly turn into animated comedies for easily-distracted and tone-deaf youth with poor eyesight eager to shovel piles of cash at them. Following an overdose of greed, Schoenberg begins a new composition he expects to title, "Endings Remain Unresolved" to be performed by his new nine-piece band, Mouth Full Of Teeth, accompanying two men who stand in man-sized trashcans and throw trash at the audience. Most cleverly, the pieces of trash are sequentially numbered and audience members struck by pieces of trash with the highest numbers receive two free tickets to the next performance where more trash will be thrown; there is no limit to the number of times an audience member can win or be hit with trash.

But then a composer who may be Pierre Boulez, in a strategy determined to avoid the blistering charge of hyperchromatism, announces his intention to compose exclusively for trick-and-roll groups, not because he is finally tired of being poor but as his most recent although hopeless effort to attract attractive companionship. No one is brave enough to assure him that his is the path least likely to reach his goal, if that truly is his goal. Meanwhile there is little doubt, certainly among composers of modern western classical music, that the performers of trick-and-roll music must eventually fade, and the facade and charade of their performances will reveal a tattered and tawdry heart whose dominant tonality is greed.

––––––––––

Ritardandos aside, Stravinsky resolves to move on from Disney to some far more successful animated-features company. After all, what he has been paid to this point hardly distracts his wives or mistresses let alone and even more urgently his seemingly numberless and thoroughly lazy children, each looking too much like Stravinsky to find gainful employment, to the annoyance and chagrin of Stravinsky. And worse, none displays the mildest curiosity about anything musical. Because of this universal absence of curiosity, Stravinsky is relieved he will only need to kill most of them to provide for his old age. Whereas Schoenberg must be prepared to exchange the profession of modern western classical music for that of professional assassin with a specialty in the elimination of composers of modern western classical music and particularly their degenerate and talentless and hopelessly snot-nosed children.

Elliot Carter notices that Stravinsky suddenly is restless, having stumbled onto a fresh crop of rubato polyrhythms just when he is tempted to compose for trick-and-roll ensembles; it is insisted by particular musicians who perform in such ensembles that they have no interest in anything resembling rubatos or polyrhythms or whatever else is believed to be music.

Even for Poulenc, the charm of composing for trick-and-roll ensembles, though profitable, is thin and odorless, tasteless, and even weightlessly mystifying. Thus Poulenc searches to find something interesting within its pseudo-genera, if only as a focus. What is it, he wonders, that convinces others, including composers of modern western classical music, that there is something that amounts to anything within the musical constrictions of trick-and-roll?

After many hours of struggle, Poulenc feels himself engorged with all of the trick-and-roll he attempts to consume as if to familiarize himself with this genre, and yet he can never digest; a musical indigestion which swirls between his ears as restless as an irritated ocean. Determined to remain obvious just for the practice, Poulenc composes trick-and-roll scores which involve whole-tone scales. Struggling to recall that he is composing music for bored and unsophisticated children and an at-best semi-conscious audience, he scribbles-over every tessitura. One more notion Gabriel Faure pounds on him about when Poulenc complains he is not being paid what his music is worth.

Faure reminds him that musicians are never paid what they are worth; often they are under-paid but occasionally they are over-paid by otherwise rapacious publishers doing the least while always paying themselves the most. This underscores the well-known saying of that forgotten composer of trick-and-roll music, Henry Cowell, that the composer with the shortest memory makes the most money. So is this the source of Poulenc's difficulty; he remembers too much of his music and too well?

Ives attempts to stay informed without surrendering to the temptation to compose along similar lines. He continues to write music as if others might read it and perhaps even play it and roughly in the way he writes it. But everyone knows that Elliott Carter is the most devious and untrustworthy among a very devious and untrustworthy bunch of trick-and-roll player/composers, pretending they compose their own sort of perverted modern western classical music and in a style that no other musician who hopes to be paid could possibly wish to imitate. Between various suspensions and inversions, such relentless trick-and-roll eventually batters the ears even of the deaf who might be otherwise regarded as fortunate.

Ives keeps all of this in mind as he ignores alternatives. As Stravinsky so often reminds him, alternatives are only apparent and never real. The score, the really big score, for each composer, has already been written and his job, and the job of every other composer of modern western classical music, is simply to play through the changes, including those parts which repeat and still sound totally crappy.

Meanwhile, Albert Roussel, just returned from his nap in the arms of death, speaks with W. C. Williams of a sudden inspiration concerning something like some festival of some sort whose vague image arises while he drifts in a state of semi-death conjuring some occasion, some event, something to bring together composers of modern western classical music in a way that all of them become more famous and also make a bit of money. Or at least enough money to cover the costs of all their drugs. Williams merely smirks confident there's no idea there even worth the hot air.

But Roussel appears intrigued that such a gathering, somehow properly financed, could at least earn them a few bags of money and composers of modern western classical music everywhere would be grateful for the attention at least as much as the money.

Word, as it inevitably does, finds Stravinsky imagining inevitable disaster. Queried about this, Shostakovich and Prokofiev shake their heads while they pummel each other and shout, certain this issue is not an issue. Milhaud refuses even to consider this doomed exercise unless Ravel or Debussy join the program. And that can never happen, at least within anyone's lifetime. Even after it is conceded that the event is unlikely to draw crowds sufficient to justify the expense, Shostakovich insists that Penderecki is as good a crowd draw as either of them and perhaps even better. Prokofiev adds that Stephan

Wolpe deserves a chance since he is even more likely to knock-out any crowd, especially as the most good-looking of modern western classical composers, of the female variety.

Weary and now annoyed over what he still thinks is his idea, Roussel is adamant; Penderecki and Wolpe can be on the program but Ravel and Debussy must be the headliners. It could only be stupid to dump headliners in favor of also-rans; more than merely stupid, that would be impossibly stupid.

Rumors drift about like bad smells. Schemes are proposed and the groups gather around Auric who flirts with a consensus announcing its opposition to every commercialism that, instead of counting musical motifs, counts boxes of cash. Ives, as can be imagined, having played and composed with the assumption that at the other end of each effort there would be at least a few humble sacks of cash, is depressed to hear this.

He turns suddenly and having failed to look bashes his head on a projecting cannon in contrary motion and then all he sees are stars. He learns that Brecht is composing what Ives assumes is one more soundtrack for one more movie with a juvenile theme. Ives avoids such work as if the last refuge for composers of modern western classical music is soundtracks for cartoons resembling the widely-despised but oddly popular Klark the Kockroach.

Ives remains curious about the conclusion that the production companies for children's cartoon programs prefer music written in the modern western classical style since it is never about anything nor resembles anything and so can never distract the child-viewers from those commercials before which they must be utterly defenseless. Ives disagrees and yet discovers an unexpected enthusiasm for being paid and frequently.

Yet Stravinsky watches because Stravinsky always watches.

And he listens.

Having returned recently from his own death, rumors about some festival of composers of modern western classical music intrigues Stravinsky. He is certain, after all, that artists, if current musicians imagine themselves artists, are eager to climb over each other's backs to advance their careers even by an instant. For that reason, whenever he hears that two so-called artists intend to collaborate, his first question is which will get the money. He remains certain that where there is competition there can never be collaboration. But something about all of this has nothing to do with money. Composers of modern western classical music lust in embarrassing ways for screaming audiences; sweating, panting, furiously flush faces turned upward, eyes glittering, sparkling, as hysterical as religious maniacs. That, all of that, is what every musician craves. The issue remains that as rich and famous as a composer may become, he will never be loved. This recognition fails to upset Stravinsky however since he writes so many ballet/operas which feature love as a plot device he is certain he knows as much about love as those who insist they have actually endured something resembling that emotion.

Having spent as much time thinking about love as anyone, Poulenc reminds himself that to advance his music writing, he must join this so-called festival's bill. If your audience isn't expanding, it is shrinking.

With that Poulenc wonders whether by composing some sort of anthem or march for this so-called festival, he would be paid twice. Charmed by this question, he reclines in a hammock strung between two large trees dressed in his cleanest underwear and reading seriously salacious material inviting his mind to drift. In this way he begins to conjure lyrics with a cadence beating two fingers of his right hand against the edge of the canvas hammock. He considers a musical theme to bind together his thoughts while thrilling his imagination. Because that is the thing he enjoys most; that sensation of a work suddenly but completely revealing its final form. Like every other composer composing such music, he knows that sensation as surely as a lover's voice. More than any particular composition, he awaits that sensation like a hunter poised beside his trap. With all of this in mind, he begins a new composition he will entitle, "Festival March Of Dotted Eighth-Notes".

————

Brecht is never amused. As he insists, he has seen this movie before. He knows what every other composer so often knows, or at least suspects, which is that any so-called festival has only one priority; earn a crapper-full of money for whoever writes the checks. If any performer makes a bit of money and becomes somewhat more famous or simply has a good time, that festival is a disaster if its organizers aren't surrounded by an ocean of bank notes.

Ives stumbles into a funk darker than any he recalls. The musician's grapevine alerts its community to the rumor of a possible festival for composers of modern western classical music. Hearing this, Ives has no choice but to plan a new composition, hopeful at least some rehearsal group will give it a run-through.

Not that such a question usually bothers him; Ives always assumes he will write well for every combination of instruments. Confident this festival is unlikely, still he realizes there is nothing else he prefers to work on which might earn some money, and is seriously unhappy there seem no other projects likely to earn any at all.

Meanwhile, with Ives's newest band (this one he calls Dogs With Small Heads since all of the band's members have dogs with small heads) he struggles to stitch together enough work to cover the month's rent. Eventually this band's three drummers put their heads together and decide that if they want the band to survive, they will need to work, and for that Ives must write new tunes which audiences will enjoy hearing them play. Unimpressed by this conclusion, Ives still understands. He likes to think well of himself yet instead he finds he is thinking about revenge. And he admits there may be nothing to resemble revenge that also brings in cash and so he finds he must make a choice; either revenge or a paycheck, but not both, or at least not both at the same time.

———————

Warners announces it is reviving the Warren The Water Buffalo cartoon series and has chosen the composer for the theme music and, to the surprise of anyone paying attention, that composer turns out to be Jan Sibelius. Automechanic to the stars, the self-taught Sibelius scratches out his compositions at his work-bench at his garage between oil changes. Except for Sibelius himself, no one thrills with this announcement. Still, Warner's fans are ecstatic with this revival so even the choice of Sibelius is acceptable if in no way exciting.

Once again deeply in debt and yet not dead although furious he has missed the chance to be paid for another Warner cartoon, Ives suspects he should contact Stevens, if the man isn't too drunk to realize his phone is ringing, or too stoned to care.

Meanwhile Shostakovich and Prokofiev suddenly have become captivated by this music festival idea. Without mentioning this to others, they are delighted simply by the prospect of leaving town, even for just a few days. Prokofiev is especially excited by the thought of wandering among trees again, an aspiration common among German composers, although Schoenberg cannot look at a tree without nausea. Shostakovich, on the other hand, is thrilled at the prospect of teaching young girls whatever instrument they like, regardless of whether he can play it.

Yet both composers know that to be successful at this festival, each will need to come up with new work, about which they begin to argue over combinations of which instruments they should compose for. Failing to decide, they consider the feeble musical themes which come to mind unable to recognize the one that will succeed.

Ives recognizes himself similarly burdened. It is clear that scrutiny will be uneven: those who have never won an award will not win any awards this time either, while it is certain that those awarded whatever has been awarded in the past will gather more here.

That's how so-called festivals and their awards work and also the reason they must not be trusted to identify or highlight anything even remotely interesting..

Ives considers a theme to organize or at least structure a work to compose for this so-called festival. Certain that whatever he submits will not win anything, he decides to submit a score few musicians will be able to read. Confident he will never win, he might still at least annoy.

As always, Stravinsky is miles ahead, his source is someone who is also organizing this overblown fantasy of a festival. Knowing as well the limitations set, including length of the composition and size and gender of every vocal chorus. Leaning back, he closes his eyes and begins to dream. This dream neither amuses nor entertains and yet leaves him intrigued. The subject of his dream shifts and then changes all together.

This dream begins when he meets someone resembling Blais Cenderas at a phonebooth and asks Stravinsky if he has any change so he can make a phone call; Stravinsky nods and reaches into his pocket but finds nothing. With this the person resembling Blais Cenderas becomes angry and asks whether Stravinsky believes he is an idiot; why tell him he has money when he has none. Stravinsky turns to discover Poulenc who insists he owes Poulenc a favor and when Stravinsky asks him why he becomes angry and storms off, replaced instantly by Darius Milhaud who reminds Stravinsky there is a composer standing on the opposite corner eager to speak with him. Stravinsky crosses the street but at the corner he finds no one. A dog nearby begins to laugh. Stravinsky is annoyed; he has never imagined how humiliated he would feel being laughed at by a dog. But as if recognizing this, the dog then describes a music composition which he insists will win a prize. Listening to the dog hum the first several notes, Stravinsky recognizes that a song-guesser has reviewed the composition but unsuccessfully. What he hears is a variation of something written long ago although it sounds nothing like it did when he wrote it. With this he wonders whether what the dog is humming may be by Milhaud unless it is a piece Stravinsky eventually balls up and tosses into his waste basket.

Albert Roussel then steps in front of the dog, nods a greeting to Milhaud and orders Stravinsky to follow him. Stravinsky asks where they are going and Roussel become furious. He turns to walk away as Stravinsky turns to follow until suddenly they are rejoined by Milhaud. Before them hangs a blood-red theater curtain. A chilling breeze swirls around them and Stravinsky guesses some message is being conveyed by this wind. He wonders if a cold wind communicates any information beyond the fact that it is cold and blowing no one any good.

Stravinsky concedes that such a breeze might convey something that resembles music, and this may have some creative value. But he concedes that aside from indicating where this breeze has been and where it is going it offers nothing useful. He suffers this dream as if something somewhere and somehow is becoming clear.

But none of that happens because that is not how dreams work.

That is, few are certain about how dreams work, but to Stravinsky's disappointment it is universally agreed that this is not that.

———

Ives pays attention though he remains unsure what he is seeing or hearing. His current project he titles, "Beyond Lies The Weirdness", an opera/ballet featuring fourteen carefully-trained dancing kangaroos backed by a twenty-two piece ensemble that includes four ultra-basses. Based on a folk melody Ives is not convinced is all that 'folk' and featuring a glass trombone quintet (two altos, two tenors and a bass), it attempts to tell the story of a young shepherd and a younger shepherdess who are in love and decide to marry but the rest of their village decide this must not happen so the young couple leave their village knowing that they will encounter miles of unrelieved weirdness ending in their deaths.

Satie hears about all of this, or least some. Every other composer of modern western classical music agrees to keep him in darkness about this festival and those monetary rewards promised. Since his most recent return from death and following the completion of a series of compositions as background for the Asian special-effects film titled, "Monster Coming", in which a boy-monster and a girl-monster fall in love and decide to marry but the various armies of the world unite to prevent this certain that if they reproduce, the end of human civilization must follow. The orchestration includes fourteen kettle-drums certain to conjure the sound of monsters coming but the piece demands many unresolved dissonances even though eventually he must resolve at least a few.

But even before he hears of this piece, Auric discovers himself nauseous considering that wall of hyperchromatism which such a composition must employ. Like other composers of modern western classical music, he experiences a panic over the dwindling supply of unresolved dissonances since so many are being resolved. Fortunately, inversions and passing tones remain in good supply.

But as is inevitable, the voices loudest in concern arise from Shostakovich and Prokofiev. Without sharing any parts of their arguments, both insist that a gathering of such a festival is a concession to the end of modern western classical music. Shostakovich especially insists that a debate must arise when an effort is made to distinguish which is or is not a composition of modern western classical music; heat and artistic anguish ensue.

Prokofiev however begins to imagine this festival differently. A gathering of avant-garde compositions will demand sophisticated and well-trained performers. With the total number of such performers limited, it is possible that most compositions will be performed poorly by less than competent performers. Thus the quality of these compositions will fail to be recognized, a dismal prospect. Stravinsky sees this crisis coming, just as Schoenberg sees Stravinsky coming.

For certain emergencies, Stravinsky keeps a box in his basement of dull but still presentable compositions usually reserved as last-minute gifts for those musicians and their companions he does not know well or fails to like much. What saves these compositions is that none is longer than two pages or scored for more than two instruments. That each is otherwise profoundly boring must not be held a criticism.

Stravinsky assumes that either Shostakovich or Prokofiev is about to challenge the very definition of modern western classical music and prepares a list of composers not accomplished enough to be mistaken for composers of such music. This responsibility no one offers or even imagines Stravinsky fulfilling, and so none are prepared to reward either. Yet Stravinsky insists he takes modern western classical music so seriously he will preserve its integrity, confident in his ability to carry out that role.

Obviously, no one agrees with Stravinsky about very much; he is an island never visited by its neighbors

Somewhere in all this and unbeknownst to others, Ives reconsiders this festival idea, suspicious such a festival will benefit no one and damage everyone. He admits to Stevens he challenges anyone to demonstrate otherwise. When Stevens returns his call insisting Ives join this festival, Ives hangs-up noisily; the foul language only comes to mind later.

––––––––––

Relieved by his return from the arms of death, Milhaud entertains only one question; if I can't take over this stupid festival idea, how can I be sure I make some money?

Like most composers of modern western classical music, any plan that brings attention to composers of modern western classical music is fine, so Milhaud wonders what attention the organizers will receive; after that he wonders how much money they might be paid. Of course, he never sees himself as self-aggrandizing or obsessed with money, unless it is money he will not be paid.

Lurking at the periphery of this musical realm, Schoenberg turns and turns, thrilled with the presence of so many young and naive composers of modern western classical music eager to die for their art. He polishes his silver hammer in anticipation of delightful assaults on the talentless. Squinting his eyes he visualizes a field of slaughter sprinkled with the unburied carcasses of composers of modern western classical music, the majority academy-trained, along with the inevitable sprinkling of autodidacts. The fact that nearly all of them also perform when not teaching adds to what has not been subtracted.

Schoenberg considers donating some sympathy to these so-called composers who care for no one other than themselves; he might even turn a blind eye as well as a deaf ear to these composers who know about or even wonder about anything beyond their bafflingly personal and thoroughly tone-deaf music; confusion proves to be the only valued emotion. As if music, like water, will float anything. So when he hears rumors about some ludicrous plan for some group performance festival, he experiences severe stomach cramps from laughing so hard. As if such a musician would do anything until a gun is put to his head or money is waved under his nose. This image thrills him as he visualizes composers of modern western classical music with brightly shining revolvers poised beside otherwise badly trained ears. Schoenberg refuses to chuckle yet struggles to resist. Determined to complete at least one more composition before he becomes dead again, he manages to scrawl "The Infamous Yoga Bathmat", based on a nauseating composition by Stravinsky; a cantata without singers performing music without songs involving music without lyrics. The piece is composed for an intrabassoon quintet augmented with a percussion ensemble that includes electrified marimba and baritone theremin. Schoenberg is especially fond of the theremin in ensemble settings since it so reminds him of the sound of those flying saucers he watches as they take off.

Auric recognizes that somehow he has fallen behind and now risks losing the thread and so fail to be invited to this musical festival he hears rumors of, even if these rumors conflict with each other over time and place, as if merely a mutually agreed upon delusion conjured to depress composers of modern western classical music. As usual Auric remains depressed by his lack of self-confidence which holds him back from composing works that would thrust him at least somewhat closer to the forefront of composers of music especially that written for Saturday morning cartoons, certainly the most lucrative of all the tv broadcasts. He considers being angry with someone although the question of who leaves him even more annoyed since he is certain of his embarrassment and fortunate in that certainty. So when he learns of a new Saturday morning children's game show to be called, "Okey-Pokey-Dokey", it feels as if he has already written the score and only needs to commit it to paper.

Can this finally be Auric's big break?

What Auric needs to consider first is the instrumentation; maybe glass trombones, lots of them but also a few intrabasoons and a theremin. Then he wonders whether there are lyrics, because if so, singers will need to have words written for them to sing. And by the way, who is paying for rehearsals?

Prokofiev and Shostakovich meanwhile also hear about this cartoon program and its need for music. They argue deep into the night about who should write the score and who the lyrics. This argument, which can only be expected, continues over several days as each assumes the other must concede even if that never happens and remains unlikely now. Shostakovich wonders whether it is time finally to give up working with Prokofiev and instead begin to collaborate with Milhaud. They went to high school together, after all, albeit to different high schools and at different times. And they both hate Schoenberg although for different reasons. Besides, Milhaud scores for glass trombones like no one Shostakovich has ever heard.

Prokofiev of course is tempted to roughly the same progress but instead considers a collaboration with Poulenc, a superb orchestrator for a baritone intrabasson choir.

Eventually Hindemith returns to life and instantly is hired by M-G-M to compose theme music for a new cartoon series based on the character from the Kafka novella titled "Sappy The Lunkhead", staring a cartoon kangaroo and his faithful wombat companion Greg, all burdened with utterly painful down-under accents. An oddly unlikely program for Australian tv broadcast to fulfill some contractual obligation, to the surprise of several, South America (all of it) expresses such enthusiasm for the program that the producers prepare a feature-length film as a preview and promotion for its Spanish-translated tv series. To Hindemith's annoyance, its theme-music must be scored for between six instrument and twelve and no musical passage continues for more than nine seconds. None of this impresses him until he recalls that these specifications are identical to those for the warmly-received cartoon series "Sock-Puppet Terror". That series, he now recalls, continues for nine seasons and his earnings cover the costs for six sets of dental braces, two college educations, one divorce and resulting alimony, and a second-hand automobile. So he considers what next to spend this money on and suddenly a vision arises; under a piercing sun, a glittering sailboat festooned with top-less females comes unbidden to his visual mind. And to his relief he fails to remember what has happened to the automobile.

Dead or otherwise, Hindemith recognizes an opportunity when it kicks him in the nuts and he is loath to let it slip away. He thinks about instrumentation and the sound of six piccolotubas—three alto, two tenor and one baritone—come to his mind. With this his imagination drifts to a mass assault by a dozen tenor drums and a trio of auto-duo-harps, that being an instrument which has intrigued him since grade school with its exotic shape and annoying, nearly ear-piercing tonality. He searches his memory for another composer of modern western classical music who has successfully scored for the auto-duo-harp and with relief no one comes to mind, or at least no one he takes seriously; composers no longer alive no longer count for anything important until they overcome their own deaths, as Nietzsche insists, especially to repay debts contracted at the rat races.

Hindemith communicates all of this to Ives and to Ives's instant fury.

Cannons and strettos and latent cadences; all are now threatened and Ives knows he will need to endure many hours of sleepless nights searching for that adequately accomplished intrabassoon player who knows the Phrygian mode, one more resource that Ives loathes.

Stopping on the street, Ives wonders what the point of any of this could be. He writes and writes and yet cannot fail to notice a thing he regularly ignores; there is a limit to everything in the universe.

Ives regularly resists most styles of despair as corrosive speculations in the short term. But occasionally he sorts his compositions and finds himself depressed. He refuses to evaluate that work, and instead simply notes its variety. More and more he puts pen to paper simply to enjoy putting pen to paper. Thus he continues to look forward to putting pen to paper and so succeeds in his most precious aspiration; he simply enjoys the work itself. He hopes without confirmation there is an audience prepared to listen to his music and waits to hear more. In the end it is all about the doing of the work itself, a moment when his pen touches that next blank sheet of paper determined to speckle it with little black dots still thrilling; moments of concentrated starshine for the ears. This, just this, thrills Ives to the point of embarrassment. In the midst of composing a quintet for five forms of cellophane packaging he entitles "Whirly-Birdy", he finds to his surprise that he does not wonder who might premier this piece or when; he is completely ensnared by the act of creative composition itself.

Anton Weber, returned from death and still thoroughly annoyed with Schoenberg for having stolen, following Weber's recent demise, his most favorite mistress, hears about this festival idea with disbelief just before he laughs, struggling to imagine any two composers of modern western classical music collaborating in some non-violent, uninsulting, and non-bitter fashion. Upon failing at that, he laughs even louder. Then stopping to catch his breath, he experiences a certain curiosity over this obviously ludicrous suggestion that a composer might engage in something resembling a festival; as if it is possible any two among them could agree on how to assemble a ham sandwich. Weber then notices his mind oscillate until he becomes vaguely nauseous, a symptom which most composers of modern western classical music value when they become comfortable with it. Yet, the more Weber turns this festival fantasy over in his mind, like sunshine gathering gravely in the east, the more that he begins to find it vaguely appealing.

Weber's discontent prods him until he recalls that Stravinsky owes him a favor, a really big one, which his memory finally retrieves. This favor, as amusing as it is embarrassing to recall, leads Weber to plan its redemption.

Stravinsky's swimming pool recordings prove more popular than even his most optimistic creditors guessed. Thus, if any sort of performance festival is considered, his presence must be assured. As Weber thinks further, he considers additional composers of modern western classical music whose participation would increase the audience. He remembers Antheil and his charming mechanical bride, and then of Bartok and his castle and his six quartets for harmocarina which are now so popular they are covered by trick-and-roll bands at high school proms several times a year.

Inside his head Weber gradually accumulates a list of composers whose recent compositions and current bands might combine in such a way that would attract an audience.

Of course and as must be expected, when Hindemith hears the outline of this goofy plan he is instantly sullen to the point of fury, in part because he easily guesses the names of composers which will be printed on the posters and flyers in large letters and which, like his own, will be printed in smaller letters. And yet on reflection he acknowledges that even printed in very small letters, at least his name will appear and large enough to be recognized. Annoyed as he is, he cannot deny the event might prove useful and even profitable.

Vaguely and unevenly, the rumor that something seriously big is afoot travels among composers of modern western classical music. At first Shostakovich and Prokofiev are furious at this news, mostly because they are certain they each should have thought of this idea even if then rejected due to its colossal stupidity. Milhaud, on the other hand, is vaguely intrigued. Mostly he wonders whether this might be the perfect occasion to premier his most recent and exciting composition titled, "The Girl In The Hooters T-Shirt", a profoundly melodramatic tone-poem with lots of the color orange in it and telling the amazing story of a girl wearing a Hooters t-shirt, scored for several intra-bassoons and numerous hand-drums.

Yet few other composers appear interested. With all of the music being played, whoever will recall any of those inevitable clunkers which, in every high-stress musical environment, must sprout like mushrooms after a rain.

Georges Auric, on the other hand, is so excited by this rumor he nearly checks himself again into a high-end rehabilitation center, his inevitable fallback strategy when under threat of abnormal excitation. Furious and depressed at being relegated to the deepest shadows of modern western classical music, the simple possibility Auric might participate in any performance festival suggests he open a second bank account since his first is unlikely to be large enough to hold all the money he must inevitably be paid.

But it is Francis Poulenc who recognizes how best to exploit this opportunity. He chooses the composition to perform and the band to perform it with based on which soloist is most likely to make the fewest mistakes, indifferent to whether that attention to the composition will prove positive or negative.

As it turns out, and to nearly everyone's surprise, the composer most excited by the prospect of this festival turns out to be none other than Arthur Honegger. He continues to compose his railroad locomotive symphonies but admits that none have gained the attention he is certain they deserve. So he is impressed by this festival idea since it is instantly obvious that it offers a chance to be heard by the fans of all those other bands. And who knows but even a brief exposure might create a few more fans and sell a few more albums. He is so curious about the value of such a festival, at least for his musical career, he begins to annoy every other composer of modern western classical music with his babbled and foggy questions.

Milhaud watches Honegger approach and looks around for a path of escape; his contempt for Honegger's stupid railroad locomotive symphonies has no limit. Yet Honegger manages to maneuver him into one more corner although not happily. He then praises Milhaud for his doubts concerning this festival and then drops the name of every composer of modern wester classical music he can think of, along with that composer's spouse or pseudo-spouse, determined to highlight every possible advantage to participation in this festival.

Milhaud becomes furious with impatient certainty that just because he can compose a railroad locomotive symphony, this upstart has a damn lot of nerve pretending to know something about Milhaud's lively current pseudo-spouse, whose name he remembers as Samatha Somethingorother, certainly a name even more baffling than any Bartok glass trombone quartet. But despite his reluctance, Milhaud begins to agree with Honegger and then begins to fantasize about his own possibly expanded audience and similarly enlarged bank account. And with all that perhaps even a revival of that glow he no longer sees in Samatha's eyes, if in fact that still is Samantha and those still are her eyes. Despite his determination otherwise, Milhaud drifts annoyingly towards collaborating with Honegger, and Honegger begins to suspect he is onto something. Yet he admits to himself the climb before him for this festival remains steep.

Time passes and Honegger finds himself standing behind Georges Auric in line to purchase tickets for a Bartok concert with his new band, Symphonic Chiffon. Without even a nod toward polite conversation, Honegger launches into a harangue about how great it would be to have a festival of composers before asking if he or Bartok plan to compose music to be performed at this festival.

Auric is startled by Honegger's sudden appearance and undisguised enthusiasm but even more by his question, mostly because he has no idea what Bartok plans, but also because this festival remains a rumor resembling a hoax and sold by the yard to delusional and desperate composers. Besides, Auric's current patron, whose name he momentarily forgets, insists that such a festival is impossible, but that even if it does happen it will draw an audience even smaller than that for your least favorite experimental silent film. Yet here stands Arthur Honegger, insisting that this festival is inevitable and every composer still breathing is composing at least one piece to premier.

Honegger then prattles about subjects of which he has no inkling while trying to sound as if he has taken entire responsibility for this festival's success. What he appears determined to convince Auric about is that despite doubts and criticisms this festival will take place. And secondly, this festival will prove wildly successful and therefore materially advantageous to all. Beyond that, it can only prove artistically profound. When Auric does not absolutely refuse to participate, Honegger is relieved and assumes his eventual participation. And as they join the crowd for this Bartok concert, he expects to ensnare two composers with one treble clef.

Yet despite being approached respectfully back stage, Bartok insists with dispiriting disdain that he will never participate in such a travesty of artistic and also financial degradation. Further, he would never tolerate any other composer of modern western classical music sharing his substantial coat-tails. Plus also he almost forgets to note he has never written anything simply to be part of some crowd of baffled and deluded and even deaf musical hacks.

Bartok does not share with Honegger the fact he has just signed an extended contract with Disney for theme music to a new cartoon series staring a friendly tarantula named Hugo and his cockroach companion Prince Ludwig. Bartok worries that participation in such a festival with annoying as well as degenerate and tone-deaf composers with their modern western classical music flying about, might jeopardize that contract as well as his audience. Spider shows and movies, after all, are suddenly the most eagerly exploited. Bartok recognizes that if he misses this chance, he is unlikely to sign another contract to compose for another spider show, no matter how popular, even while cockroach cartoon shows are now a dime a dozen and therefore doomed to oblivion along with whoever composes their music.

But a more formidable line of resistance is asserted by Stravinsky.

Due to his advanced age and enormous wealth, unless it is something else, to his deep regret Stravinsky has participated in similar pretentious exercises and is burned on every occasion. Even without knowing anything else about this so-called festival, he already smells the piles of rotting garbage, the overflowing toilets, and odorous smelling bodies; plus the sprained ankles, the split lips, and the various forms of chemically-induced psychoses. A profoundly stupid fact remains; in the end, no one will ever, even beyond the distant future, be paid in money for this exercise. Besides, Stravinsky's performance schedule is so overloaded he has no need for still another job. But he shakes his head as he also notes that he knows no other composer of modern western classical music who is not also desperate for paying work.

And here a crack appears that Honegger recognizes he can exploit. After congratulating Stravinsky on his swimming pool performance, piles of wealth and sterling collection of mistresses he launches into a diatribe on the disturbing absence of material success of composers who resemble him and for which he should be concerned.

Stravinsky falls asleep over accounts of misery and misunderstanding among his counterparts but then the names of Shostakovich and Prokofiev conjure images of that tiny apartment the two must share. Honegger casually mentions the name Aquatain Submarine, the notorious but also beloved master felxophone artist. Respected as a last survivor of that glorious generation of flexophonists, Submarine struggles to squeeze each last bank note from these delusional composers of modern western classical music; if you can merely play a guitar or even a harmocarina, you can make a living; or at least this is what Stravinsky insists to every composer who will listen; if you've got a union card and an instrument, where is your problem? With the completion of his most recent ballet/opera entitled, "Micro-Waves", concerning the adventures of a corps of miniature naval nurses and their bizarre but thrillingly erotic hijinks, Stravinsky is not surprised that even Warner's is dizzy with interest. Having finally fine-tuned his new de-syncopater, Submarine is certain he will perform the music of any and every one of these youngster-composers even better than they can possibly imagine.

———————

Hearing rumors from certain sources of some festival involving music, Milhaud is torn over whether to be excited or insulted. It occurs to him that this might be his best and perhaps even his last chance to try out his newest band (this one he calls Danny and the Whole-Tone Suicides) with some of his music compositions for those circuses with big-tops which still travel about even if not for very much longer. For that reason, if he hopes those compositions are ever heard by anyone other than the musicians who practice them, this festival offers a final shot.

With this possible festival now threatening, even after trashing their most recent hotel room, Shostakovich and Prokofiev make public their agreement to participate in what increasingly appears a possibly popular event. Honegger is encouraged by this even as he doubts he'll hear from Schoenberg. Alban Berg, on the other hand, announces that in anticipation of this so-called festival, he will journey to an island so remote even he won't know where he is. Among those who know him well, none finds this promise especially persuasive let alone likely while all assume eventually he won't be able to refuse without losing money. Composers of modern western classical music are certain Weber will agree and Berg will do the same.

And then there is Albert Roussel. He is eager to throw bombs, or at least non-exploding rocks if that is all he has, to prevent this festival from happening. Yet secretly he knows this world of music continues to change and filthy trick-and-roll is just one more sign.

Thinking all of this, Roussel is compelled to agree that this festival, as bogus and baffling as it sounds, may be his very last chance to capture the attention of that far younger audience he is assured he must pursue. He has nearly finished a sonata chock-o-block with double-time arpeggio-like elements and entitled, "Eating Better Electrically", about a boy-electrician and a girl-electrician who fall into what they both spend three acts insisting is love, even while despite urgent gestures and panicked efforts their cascade of love-sparks simply never appears. If Roussel cannot hire enough intrabasson players he'll need to substitute some group of trombonophone artists; he is confident that at least those will give each performance some kick!

Despite Roussel's annoyance, when Honegger finally meets with Ives to describe his plan for the festival, Ives's response startles even Honegger. It appears Honegger has caught Ives at a particularly good time, unless it is an especially bad time but which Ives decides to ignore. Ives has begun to hire a new band he calls the Slaughter-House Five Plus Twelve; a seventeen-piece ensemble with numerous intrabassons plus also four glass trombones and so much more. He insists that each player accurately play at least three instruments, thus offering the widest musical pallet Ives has written for. And finally, having purchased his own de-syncopator, he is hard at work on his newest sinfonietta entitled, "Unicorn Stampede", the story of a boy unicorn herder and a girl unicorn herder who fall in love and decide to marry but their respective unicorns refuse to allow it on some obscure principle having to with virginity.

So this festival offers Ives a chance to perform his most ambitious compositions for a non-dead, or perhaps only marginally comatose, audience. Using his own de-syncopator, he begins a new composition for tenor modulator, an instrument so difficult to compose for that few since J. S. Bach have ever bothered and even then with limited success, especially since an accomplished tenor modulator player is usually so old as to have already been relegated to the appropriate underfunded public facility for such otherwise burdensome individuals.

Having wasted so much of his youth and early adulthood being dead, Paul Hindemith recognizes that if he hopes to catch up with modern western classical music, this so-called festival is his best and perhaps also his very last chance. But to take full advantage, he must hire an entirely new band since all of the members of his old bands are now playing in other bands. But more critically, he needs to come up with several entirely new compositions and the funkier the better. Although only briefly, he is tempted to ask Roussel for the loan of his de-syncopator since Ives has already refused. Hindemith then puts pen to paper and experiences an illumination whose title comes to him as, "Greed Is Hell", a de-syncopated ballet/opera in three movements depicting in three successive scenes in the life of a bank manager who begins the ballet/opera happy and ends the ballet/opera unhappy. Its swamp of entangled financial chicanery triggers peculiar emotions as well as demonstrates several perverted principles and practices of business accounting which supply the narrative thread, all of it in service to the old saying; nothing good ever happens inside a bank. A work of startling freshness and violence, Hindemith is confident it will fit perfectly within the otherwise unannounced and unspecified ethos of this festival.

Berg, meanwhile, fronting his newest band, Liars for Jesus, recognizes this festival is his last chance to premier his most recent composition, "Turning Wine Into Gin", a grupetto scored for a dozen harmocarinas accompanied by an as-yet unnamed rhythm section. Berg has imagined a composition festooned with artificial harmonies, tetrachordal groupings along with, and certainly not scrimping on, glissandi out the wazoo plus certain delightful countermelodies.

Honegger is pleased by the progress of his newest railroad symphony composition but even more, the brightening prospects for this festival. And he is relieved at how quickly he recruits other composers of modern western classical music. Finally he confronts Ravel and Debussy.

At first, he tries to convince himself this is no more than a bump in the road; a mild distraction with limited implications. But days pass and these French knuckleheads remain silently intransigent as well as French.

Honegger eventually convinces himself that of course Ravel and Debussy will participate. Considering how long they've been dead one should assume they will at least enjoy the fresh air and exercise, especially since being dead there is no way they could have worked up any new compositions. Besides, they won't be asked to do anything except stand by smiling and handing out awards to the unworthy. And considering the composers and musicians expected to attend over those three days of the festival, someone inevitably will perform one of their compositions even if it demands a fistfight or even worse, all certainly to the audience's delight.

But things become more complicated with Brecht's arrival. Of course, Brecht is not Busoni and neither is he F. M. Marinetti. When Brecht isn't dead he is snowed under with paperwork for his dry-cleaning empire. In fact he is regularly so busy with paper he fails to think about composing modern western classical music. But then his invitation to this festival arrives.

Being a successful businessman as well as avant-garde composer, Brecht, recognizes instantly how this opportunity will help his music-writing career, but even more, despite its silliness, how this festival will also help his business since even composers and performers of modern western classical music need their clothes cleaned from time to time. And it happens he has several compositions in rough draft he can quickly polish and whose performance should prove appealing. In particular, one composition entitled, "Aliens in Pajamas", in which a boy-alien is about to celebrate his birthday and his alien girlfriend buys him pajamas as a gift, but seeing them he is instantly disappointed although tries to appear pleased but his girlfriend recognizes his disappointment and whips out her ray-gun shooting him dead, certain there are more boy-friends where that one came from and at least one will be pleased to receive her charming pair of pajamas. Brecht now faces the question of where he will find twelve intrabasson players ready to travel with their very delicate instruments. His new business manager/accountant named Franz Kafka (not that Franz Kafka, but a cousin) insists this will be his most popular composition ever, especially since none of his other compositions has ever proved to be even vaguely popular. For this reason his prediction appears as risky as a sunrise; Brecht is content to grasp at every straw floating by.

Word of what is gradually becoming Honegger's music festival circulates in wider and wider orbits despite responses that range from annoyed indifference to active hostility; the moment word gets out that this or that composer has agreed to participate, opinions change. Thus, Antoine Artaud initially mocks this festival but then in his role as promoter of several successful festivals for trick-and-roll bands announces his lucrative participation; he has already decided how much money he will be paid and so will soon bank even more money than Stravinsky.

Then, at least according to Milhaud, Olivier Messiaen insists a choir of musicians and one of birds are equally blessed and equally a blessing, over which Schoenberg simply laughs corrosively. Then again Schoenberg is always eager to share a joke, even if it is not funny, about some other composer. What leaves him annoyed are those composers of modern western classical music whining about how little money there is for them to share. As far as Schoenberg figures it, if there were half as many composers, there would be twice as much money. Ezra Pound, returning from the failure of his dental floss farm, remains unconvinced even if he is prepared to accept anyone's check in exchange for doing literally anything.

Ives remains doubtful this so-called festival can actually take place but more, and more seriously, those who agree to be unconvinced participants will be paid much. He too easily envisages days of music followed by decades of poverty, and this notion leaves him utterly pissed off. He is certain that in a truly just world he would be paid as much as Stravinsky, and perhaps even more. He wonders then if any song-guessers will perform at this festival and instantly thinks of Georges Auric. Of course, competitive song-guessing remains controversial with representatives of various techniques stepping forward and demanding opportunities to perform, and several academic song-guessers even speak out in defense of their practice although always unsuccessfully.

Uncertain his song-guessing will influence the judges and earn him a slot on the playbill. Auric completes his most recent cantata entitled, "Night of the Living Shareholders", wherein a boy stock broker and a girl stockholder fall in love and decide to marry but find themselves suddenly surrounded by a coven of vampire lawyers representing zombie shareholders who pounce wrestling them to the ground and sucking dry their wallets; Auric is morally certain this cantata will find an audience. Expecting to increasing its appeal he composes it in the hyperPhrygian mode—that mode which is startlingly Phrygian—while adding barcaroles constructed to please the ladies.

A sort of hypochondria begins to circulate among the composers of modern western classical music; its primary manifestation is the compulsive waving of both hands held above the head but in opposite directions. Whether seated or standing or even in recline, with no warning, the victim begins to wave his arms almost as if he is standing before a musical ensemble attempting to conduct. The most famous conductors find this behavior charming even while choking back the obvious insult. After all, conducting any musical ensemble resembles the herding of earthworms. To even the most insensitive, this resemblance is so uncanny it is dispiriting.

Honegger watches from what he believes is a safe distance as complications accumulate. He feels himself standing at the foot of a very high mountain which is becoming higher as its peak offers the answer to a question he forgets he has asked.

At this moment, Stravinsky endures a crisis of confidence.

———————

Stravinsky's newest band, Psychotic Obstruction, has just begun a two-week gig at Tommy's Top-Heavy Tavern. Having for a very long time high-lighted his piano performances by crushing his pianos with his hugely powerful hands despite the enormous burden put upon the local elephant population, Stravinsky wonders if this festival provides his chance to display a change of heart or at least a change of practice. But also he wonders what that decision might mean to his most loyal supporters. Will they drop like flies or flee like rats, or cheer and applaud and purchase more of his unattractive and over-priced t-shirts? Even his new booking agent and business manager, Walter Benjamin, shrugs with his confusion over this question.

But yet and still, this festival appears on the verge of actually take place.

To the surprise of many, it is Edgar Varèse who truly gets the ball rolling. After numerous discouraging efforts of several unemployed but otherwise enthusiastic composers of modern western classical music, he locates a distant farm of many acres and convinces its owners that what their community needs more than anything is a music festival featuring famous and popular composers of modern western classical music, from which they will produce a hit album plus also screen a popular motion picture recording of their individual performances. Following all of this their community must become famous everywhere and forever.

Described in this way including all of the appropriate lies, the civic authorities involving this farm become excited and even ask what they can do to make the event a success. Varese assures them that what this festival will really need is toilets, lots and lots of toilets. Leaving their meeting, Varese realizes he has a great idea for a new composition.

For reasons yet to be explained, Debussy and Ravel stop speaking to each other. While this is not the first time nor likely the last, yet it appears so certain their rift will fail to find its patch before this gathering festival, that even their closest friends can only shake their heads. Milhaud, closer to Ravel than to Debussy, cannot recall when they have had a more acrimonious dispute. While both composers hail from an earlier generation, the younger generation of composers remains respectful of their music even when they snicker behind their backs about their likely sexual inadequacy and other afflictions of composers of modern western classical music accumulated over obnoxious but irresistible antiquity.

At about this time Georges Auric, dead until quite recently and therefore recognizing he's getting a rather late start for this festival, begins to assemble another new band he plans to call Derek and The Behavioralist, the players from his last band having been snatched up by other composers of modern western classical music. Certain parties advise him to hire T. S. Elliot as his band's accountant and business manager, but Auric has been around the block often enough and so is certain he has several better ideas.

But it is Busoni, more recently dead than not, who snares the contract with RCA to record the festival. With this, the battle for rights to the film of the festival begins; Disney and Warners assume they have the inside track since neither takes M-G-M seriously; the flurry of checks drifting about written in large denominations even attracts the attention of the print media, an otherwise inevitably baffled crowd, and much to the eventual regret of Busoni.

Forces beneath the musical surface continue to roil and churn.

Ives noodles about among the other composers hopeful of discovering who plans to attend this so-called festival to ask what benefit that composer's participation will offer. He knows he needs the exposure and his band needs the practice but most of all there needs to be a paycheck. And now he hears speculation of that compilation album which Busoni has contracted but then Ives is startled by rumors of a feature-length movie as well. He scratches his head as he so often does, certain these are things he should understand or at least anticipate and so this unfair bafflement is well-earned.

His phone calls to several former band members either go unanswered or to voicemail. As always, he would rather be composing the most annoying music he can imagine although he must never forget he has an apartment and a car, both of which suck away his money like water in the desert. And his band's musicians splash money about as if it belongs to them. So all of this reminds him his music must not to be too crazy or soon he won't be making any music at all. At this moment he reminds himself, as if he must, that he's already not making any money. And even his friend Stevens finds his unappetizing music indigestible and so his words of concern always fall on deaf and even occasionally dead ears.

And yet, despite all of this confusion and the conflicts, this festival idea appears to be gaining serious even if unlikely support. Antonie Artaud, writing for one more duplicitous music industry rag, insists that if this festival ever takes place, album sales alone will astonish even the pseudo-experts, fortunately but also unfortunately for modern western classical music. But Ives refuses to wonder further; if that prediction turns out only partly accurate, he will eagerly snatch at whatever cash happens to drift by.

———————

Honegger avoids thinking about security for this festival even though there are fanatics and religious music isolationists desperate to assassinate every composer of modern western classical music. He wonders how many composers of modern western classical music this world can afford to lose, and he is bemused by the total.

Francis Poulenc returns from the dead once more thoroughly pissed-off; had he known about this festival he would never have allowed himself to die, or at least would have complained loudly. As it is, he is certain his new band, the Antiquated Neurologists, just on general principal should head-line this so-called festival. But with his death, even if temporary, his band's members scatter to the four winds. Even his arraigner, Neal Cassidy, someone Poulenc never trusts let alone likes, absconds with the little money Poulenc keeps in the bank, along with and far worse, a stack of his band's arrangements and compositions. Worse even than that, Cassidy fails to get this own band any bookings. So this so-called festival may be Poulenc's last chance to get that band back together for some money and even pay-off some of his musicians; not all or even most but certainly several.

At this moment, the theme music for the new children's cartoon show intended for adults that Poulenc agrees to write for Disney titled, "Cooking French People At Home" explodes within his mind until he stumbles and nearly falls. Certain he needs to form a new band for the series, which will be called "Life Is Short And Not That Pretty" (Disney's title, not his) he makes many phone calls.

Himself never a joiner, Erik Satie watches all of this silliness from the sidelines with a bemused smile optimistic he will forget everything he hears, eventually.

Satie's most recent band, Weirdo Shit Bru-Haha, breaks up some time before and he basks in the blessed relief he will never see those musical barbarians again nor ever need to write any of them a check except if beclouded within some horrendous trick-and-roll hell. Of course and as he admits, it has been a while since he could write any check without risking jail time, incarceration being even worse than death. Yet he continues to compose, not because anyone pays attention or even appears curious let alone distracted by his compositions. Instead, this new band he forms, if there is a next time, must have something to rehearse and screw-up in public performance to Satie's inevitable yet still infuriated chagrin. Satie insists he knows better and somehow will use that knowledge eventually.

Antheil and his mechanical bride collaborate on a composition they are convinced is entirely new. After several years working as a roofer, Antheil awakes one morning to discover he has spent his life both wrong and backward; if he ever hopes for a life of wealth and respect, he must compose modern western classical music and a lot of it. His mechanical bride is less certain and silently even suspects the opposite. But as a bride, even a mechanical one, she knows her responsibility is to go along or find another young and virile former-roofer.

Antheil, however, has never been without resources even though he has no idea how one goes about actually playing a piano, any piano, and otherwise use its resources to their best advantage. So he does what he always does when he is bemused by perplexity; he calls Bruno Maderna. Head coach of the local soccer team, a sport Antheil hates as much as all of the other sports he hates, he values Maderna's ability to inspire when he isn't being a pain in the ass.

And Maderna always offers the same advice; in order to get there, you need to leave here.

So when Antheil's call to Stravinsky goes unanswered, Madern is the only person he tells since Maderna always pretends to be curious to hear what that Great Man might say.

When finally reached on the phone, Stravinsky tells Antheil something that might prove useful; he tells Antheil to hire as many intrabasson players and piccolotuba players as he can afford. When Antheil asks why, Stravinsky just smiles over the telephone. Antheil knows he should never trust that smile, even over the telephone, except that this time he does.

After trashing one more hotel room, Shostakovich and Prokofiev are no longer speaking to each other, even at rehearsals. Instead, members of the band pass notes to one or another along with whatever response, and lately those responses are brief. The rest of the band awaits the moment when those responses evaporate into silence. Already the band's arranger, Karl-Heinz Stockhausen, is running the band and without a word to either Shostakovich or Prokofiev. He appears certain he knows what this band needs and even more how this festival will benefit modern western classical music as well as himself. Plus, since he'll soon be in the market for a new job, running this band, even badly, should help that search.

Bartok remains certain all of this talk about some festival of modern western classical music is both delusional and a waste of precious time if not also over-priced staff paper. If anything, for those baffled enough to pay the absurd ticket price and then actually show-up, the boredom factor will go through the roof. And then he has an idea for a new intrabasson quartet which he shares with no one until his lawyers have approved.

Within the world of modern western classical music, the participation of lawyers continues to expand, unfortunately. Ives himself considers the possible employment of a lawyer and whether such assistance will add to his resources or reduce them. He remembers that even Stravinsky from time to time finds the participation of a lawyer useful. Following the publication of his pseudo-autobiography with soundtrack, "Clean Out Your Ears", and Arron Copelan's subsequent claim that he has composed an identical piece he entitles, "Diary of An Ear-Worm", the word 'lawyer' raises its very ugly head. Although both compositions employ a seven-part rondo followed by a brief hemiola, Stravinsky's lawyer, Andre Breton, argues that those two compositions can never be regarded as similar. Of course and eventually the litigation collapses; the judge for the trial disappears. It is later reported she has begun to compose modern western classical music herself since it is so easy and obviously profitable. Stravinsky is furious and for days after looks about frantic in search of someone, anyone, he can sue or otherwise punch very hard in the nose.

Shostakovich and Prokofiev, in an industry-starling reversal, insist to the musical press that despite rumors otherwise, their newest band, Ten-Cent Nickles, is so highly-trained it will play anything tossed its way. Hearing this, Zubin Meta, a new member of the musical press, asks if they plan to attend the upcoming music festival, and both laugh insisting they have already composed all of the music any band could need. Meta himself laughs as their attorney, Jacques Lipshitz, steps forward offering his business card informing him he should prepare to be measured for a new law suit and two pairs of pants. Shostakovich and Prokofiev acknowledge in a subsequent interview that attorneys have become so common among composers that piano lessons are now part of the curriculum for attorneys-in-training. Meta remains unimpressed; what can any musician mean to any lawyer except money?

———————

Honegger presses on with this festival, increasingly certain the moment is approaching when composers of modern western classical music will find the audience they dream of. And once the film of this festival is released, even those who are not fans of modern western classical music will recognize what each of these composers looks like, so that when encountered at the supermarket or at the rat races or on the subway or even in a crowded bar, strangers can walk right up to one and pretend they know something about music after which they can claim feelings of deep friendship and admiration of their genius or, conversely, insult and berate them insisting their compositions are stupid or horrible and certainly corrupting the youth before then trying to borrow money, a certain way of creating the appearance of a personal bond, as if such a thing is useful when attempting to borrow money from a musician.

Concerning the progress of this festival; the logistics, it turns out, are baffling and infuriating and Honegger's many phone calls are frantic and go on forever. First, he decides that if they don't offer any food at this festival, they won't need nearly so many toilets. Then he realizes that if part of the cost of admission is to provide a flashlight when the patron displays his ticket, the festival won't need so much electricity for lights. Plus also, if anybody gets sick—well, Honegger will think of something. Besides, while he expects a good crowd, he does not see any chance so many fans will arrive that a medical emergency will prove a problem.

Albert Roussel, also having recently returned from being dead again, is busily putting the finishing touches on his most recent opera/ballet entitled, "Ghosts In Love" for a glass trombone quartet and intrabassoon orchestra, wherein a boy ghost and a girl ghost fall in love but, because they are ghosts and without bodies, they don't exactly have a lot of that sort of fun, and the less said about this the better. Completing this composition, he looks around for a quartet plus a few unemployed dancers willing to work below scale to rehearse the piece even if the music appears difficult or boring. To his own surprise, he finds this composition even more annoying than boring, and with that reminds himself that hardly anyone writes for the glass trombone any more so promotion of the composition should prove a breeze.

With this festival-thing seeming to become more likely, even though Roussel is as contemptuous as he is annoyed, he recognizes this may finally provide him the chance to return to writing circus music, that genre he hasn't been paid to compose in since authorities outlawed circuses as demonic and also unhealthy distractions for young people constantly vulnerable to its uselessness and its power to confuse and distract which tempts them to mock their elders.

What is instantly obvious, the instrument Roussel really enjoys composing for is the crocophone, a musical wind-device made up largely of overlapping hides of alligators and crocodiles, layered diagonally, sandwiching additional layers of broken glass around a pig's bladder; sort of like a football but more musical. The crocophone dates to the Middle Ages and much of the music composed in that period has survived although in incomplete or corrupted copies (hardly anyone writes anything new for that instrument). Thus Roussel can expect that his will be the only such composition on the festival play-bill composed for that instrument and so his work should attract a lot of unwarranted and even annoying curiosity. Happily for the world of crocophone-players, Roussel will turn out to be wrong.

Meanwhile, and despite his work to prepare for what he still hopes will be a grand festival, Honegger completes one more of his railroad locomotive symphonies; this one he titles, "Mogul 2-6-0" after a pet dog of his childhood.

———————

Stravinsky stands in the center of the spacious and bright ballroom of his mansion admiring his four glittering new baby-grand pianos just delivered by those strong but friendly young men from Baldwin piano company. He and these muscular young men have become especially friendly since they deliver new pianos to his home roughly every month. He turns to admire his brand-new pianos as he considers this so-called music festival and wonders before he looks down at his enormous, nearly monstrous and powerful hands (each nearly large enough to span half a keyboard), wondering how anyone could imagine such a music festival without his participation. But then he grins, certain that of course no one can. Yet still, Stravinsky struggles with an infuriating sense of annoyance.

He has heard the rumors that both Shostakovich and Prokofiev plan to participate. So he wonders whether they assume his own participation. He considers starting a rumor that he will not attend, and instead perform several of his greatest hits at a different venue. But he will compose secretly for this festival and have his band, The Circular Firing Squad, perform something that kicks such serious ass it rattles the musical universe. Not that he has much difficulty in that regard; his compositions always kick ass or he doesn't bother with them. Besides, Stravinsky recalls his appearance with Roussel at the Club Bandwidth and how no one made money except those cretin t-shirt vendors, and they grumbled so loudly they nearly drowned out the music being performed. And Stravinsky remembers with embarrassment how drunk Roussel became and his attempts to punch Stravinsky in the nose leading to a stumble followed by a fall so awkward Roussel was unable to compose modern western classical music for almost a week.

Yet Stravinsky knows that Roussel never joins in anyone's musical performance without a plan. Even knowing that Ravel and Debussy have fallen out as friends, Stravinsky knows them both well enough to know that neither will appear without something new and fresh and sparkling with hyperchromatic quarter-tones laid over a rainbow of microtonal arpeggios in each back pocket. Those sly Frenchmen are devious and overly-musical and thus untrustworthy. It is simple enough to join a music performance, but Stravinsky knows it is far more difficult to get out of one.

Francis Poulenc, recently returned from being dead, realizes he must assemble a new band if he hopes to take advantage of this apparent festival but he is having little success or even fun. And worse, since he does not yet know which musicians playing which instruments to hire forming his new band, he really can't begin to write new work. He has several ideas which appear clever and even vaguely interesting that include a newly-written medley of several of his tunes no one has found interesting; he considers titling the piece, "Terracotta Morons", although he has no idea why since that title refers to nothing Poulenc has ever even wondered about.

Satie, on the other hand, remains tormented by doubts. Spending a weekend on the telephone speaking with every composer of modern western classical music who responds, he wonders if this festival is just one more baloney and bluster sandwich. After all, he has spent time in his musical laboratory hunched over his musical microscope in close analyses of an extensive sampling of compositions of modern western classical music and from this he recognizes with perfect certainty that modern western classical music is about to die. Since this is scientific and therefore irrefutable, Satie endures a remarkable relief his research assures him that participation in this festival will make absolutely no difference to anyone about anything.

———————

Paul Hindemith returns from the dead and heads instantly to the rat races confident that in the midst of death he recognizes those rats about to win the next six races. Still not yet completely undead, he places his bets and before his afternoon is half-over he is entirely broke. By the time he returns to his apartment he has decided that as ludicrous as it must be, he so needs the money that he has no choice but to join this festival. Yet to be included in this festival he'll need a band to front which he does not yet have. And in order to have a band he will need money and a lot of it. So, his first step to this festival is to find out who to borrow money from and how much he will need. But since every other composer of modern western classical music is also looking for money, he knows this will not prove easy. Hindemith opens a file-folder optimistic he still has several compositions that only need some polish to sound presentable.

Still, every conversation Hindemith has with Honegger leaves him depressed. Regardless of how much he borrows, that amount may still not be enough. Then inadvertently he learns of the recent dispute between Shostakovich and Prokofiev and wonders whether either of them could be convinced to collaborate. After all, he still has a nice stack of music arrangements never performed. Beyond that, Hindemith is confident that given the time to transpose any parts for instruments not already written into the arrangement, they will sound fine. He does not yet know who his partner might be, but he is feeling certain he will find one.

Both Ives and Stravinsky skirmish although over vastly different issues. As Ives struggles to decide which instruments to compose for, Stravinsky wonders which pianos in his collection he can sacrifice on the altar of modern western classical music at a festival where no one may show up. He then has an idea that startles even him; form a band that mixes players of modern western classical music with players of trick-and-roll. He then recalls that he still has the telephone number for that drummer for the trick-and-roll band, Rhonda and the Towelettes. And thinking even further, he recalls that he has an arrangement for a new concerto grosso entitled, "The Check Never Arrives", which he decides he can rescore for a trick-and-roll band. In fact, the more he thinks about this, the more excited he becomes. Especially he is tempted by the possibility of a younger—in fact, much younger—audience that will discover a taste for his work, and who knows but he and his band might even enter the trick-and-roll hall of fame. After all, how many composers of modern western classical music can claim the same?

A brief phone call dispels whatever it is that befouls Stravinsky's mind; most noxious, the roar of laughter through the telephone line from that trick-and-roll drummer whose name Stravinsky will no longer be obliged to recall and is relieved thereby.

This risible response amounts to the obvious assertion that trick-and-roll has no need of anyone involved in modern western classical music, whereas modern western classical music will die several putrid and noxious deaths without the aid of trick-and-roll. With this, the drummer hangs up and Stravinsky can only shrug; what else can one expect from a drummer?

Still and without help from any drummers or other trick-and-roll players, Stravinsky recognizes an idea for a new composition for octet of glass trombone, intrabasson and piccolotuba he'll title, "What's Wrong With Dead People". Instantly he sees this as the perfect composition to premier at the music festival. So his next question asks how to structure the piece so that he will not need any drummers and instead will get by with a couple of hyperharp players. Then he wonders whether this composition might work even better with the addition of two pianos, both of which Stravinsky would play himself and simultaneously. This would also provide the chance to destroy two pianos in the same performance and to the undoubted hysteria of his always hysterical audience.

Now that Stravinsky finally takes this festival and his participation in it seriously, he wonders just how best to make that announcement. But he is also startled by his enormous relief that he will no longer need to take seriously those pretentious, annoying and bafflingly but noxiously wealthy and thereby self-important trick-and-roll players.

———————

Brecht is finally annoyed with all of this talk about some boondoggle of a music festival. As for the idea that Ferruccio Busoni would spend even five minutes in the same room with Edgar Varese is so ludicrous that Brecht nearly forgets to laugh. Still, he sighs and shakes his head. Ready to admit how unlikely such a collaboration might be, he recognizes that modern western classical music cannot survive otherwise. And even more terrifying, there is the likelihood that when that style of music disappears. hardly anyone will notice

Without realizing it, Ives comes to the same conclusion. But unlike Brecht, he sees reasons, vague and obscure, for optimism. First, if certain composers restrain themselves and find a way to play nicely together, sharing things like musical arrangements and instruments and even performers, this so-called festival might accomplish something useful. But all of that will demand certain conditions, as Ives also recognizes. After all, how many times can one roll the dice and expect the same number to come up? Still worse, admitting how unlikely any of this is, what will result if all of these preparations are made and no audience appears?

As Ives wonders further about this, he decides that the total number of fans who attend is less important than the number who see the movie plus how many buy the soundtrack album. And so, Ives privately suspects how crucial this festival may be for the future of modern western classical music, if such a thing can be imagined. With an aroma of disaster drifting about, Ives calls Wallace Stevens hopeful he is awake and sober and so can consider more than one question at a time. Regarding the unsettled nature of this musical world surrounding him, Ives fears his best bet is to do nothing except complete his newest composition, "Dippsy Noodles", a score for a dozen instruments including piccolotuba, glass trombone, and intrabassoon, but without drums of any sort. He recognizes that the more specific one is the more likely one will be wrong and therefore become disappointed and depressed.

––––––––––

Francise Poulenc swears to himself and his wife and to everyone he owes money to, that he will never again cross the threshold to the rat races. The only reason he is attending today and losing every cent he possesses is not because he enjoys losing money, but despite knowing in advance he will lose every race, our universe of modern western classical music asserts that anything, absolutely anything, may happen, including that one of his rats finishes in the money.

Still, he is not delusional. He recognizes that his musical status is not high, but with a successful performance that status will change because it must; that's how these things work.

Honegger, on the other hand, continues to cross and recross the city attempting to recruit every composer of modern western classical music he can convince to open their door that they must attend this music festival. After several hours of this exercise he decides that a lunch is in order and goes to his favorite greasy spoon called the Greasy Spoon where every meal is served with a greasy spoon. Crossing the threshold, he recognizes sitting at the counter and hunched over a cup of coffee and with a red aluminum ashtray filled by a pile of cigarette butts stubbed out at his right, György Lukács. At that moment Honegger recalls that Lukács's most recent comic film, "Landmines For Lunatics", is so poorly received that riots result in physical injuries and police action, all heavily documented by the local press. Lukács appears to be fighting a hangover and not winning. This suits Honegger just fine because he has an idea. After asking Lukács about his health and commiserating over the fate of his film, Honegger asks if he has plans for his next film project and is silently delighted when Lukács merely shrugs.

Casually and even indifferently, Honegger describes the music festival the composers of modern western classical music are organizing. He assures Lukács arrangements move along before mentioning the recording of the festival's musical performances for an elaborate two-disc set. Lukács nods along as if he might be paying attention. Honegger then muses aloud over the possibility it might prove profitable to also film these performances for a commercial release. But even before he finishes the sentence, Lukács turns to look at him as if suddenly less hungover. Honegger realizes that now he simply needs to wait. When Lukács turns to ask how much the job will pay, Honegger leans back and smiles.

Lukács lights another cigarette and orders another cup of coffee asking how large his crew will be and what equipment will be available and have they put money aside for post-production. Finally he asks who his sound man will be. Honegger tells him that Olivier Messian has agreed to help. At this, Lukács half-stands and in a loud voice announces he'll have nothing to do with any project Messian with his stupid bird calls gets his filthy fingers into.

Expecting this, Honegger, appears startled and asks what difference it will make, to which Lukács responds that Messian adds bird-calls to every project he participates in and so destroys it. Honegger fails to think of another film director both so broke and also so desperate for a project to get himself back into the public eye, even if that public is limited to fans of modern western classical music. He explains that whatever else, Messian will work dirt-cheap and yet do just as he's told and well enough. Besides, he argues, when he has finished the soundtrack, they can fine-tune things in post-production. Snarling that he's heard all this before, Lukács insists he will only participate with the promise he will have exclusive rights to final cut.

Honegger, of course, has no power to make such a promise and so agrees gleefully, eager for the word to get the out that Lukács will do the film of the festival's performances.

With all of this seemingly nailed down, Honegger is eager to revisit those composers skeptical of this festival, ready to assure Lukács's participation in the film and certain that with this news more composers will recognize there is a project here to earn them some money, or at least cover the costs of show-ing-up. For once and perhaps the only time in their lives, these composers will see their faces on the big screen, a thing they can tell family and friends as well as the many people they owe money to without embarrassment. With this, Honegger finally can proceed with confidence, and so he does.

Preparation for this festival now moves forward and very quickly.

But just then, Shostakovich and Prokofiev announce they will no longer perform together or rehearse together or live together or even speak to each other, the unfortunate result of having trashed one more motel room. In a mutual and simultaneous statement, they announce that they will no lon-ger even appear on the same playbill together. Several composers of modern western classical music pretend regret and offer condolences while secretly delighted. Ravel and Debussy on the other hand, express disappointment. Their plan had been to announce their own reunion just before the festival with the hope that gesture will stimulate additional sales. But with this news, their announcement is suddenly no longer even vaguely interesting. In fact, the announcement appears so infuriating they are tempted to not reunite, even if this leaves at least a few composers seriously confused. Particularly Ravel, who is usually so furious he is tempted to compose something radical enough to cast the work of every other composer of modern western classical music into the deepest shade. But it is Darius Milhaud who finds himself suddenly near to overflowing with bits and pieces of music within his head eager to being combined into work that a musician might mistake for music.

Very much like his embarrassing idol, Charles Ives, Milhaud begins to compose a work he is certain others can only hear exactly the way he does, even though of late he has felt battered with self-doubt. This festival finally seems a good idea and perhaps even a ton of fun along with the added pos-sibility that some composers, maybe even several, stand a chance to make de-cent money. But Milhaud still worries. Suppose, despite his confidence along with the enthusiasm of others, this so-called festival turns into something much closer to a disaster and the crowd of attending young people, or at least youngish people, never finally arrives. Or worse, the crowd finds itself aban-doned, without food or water or any form of medical care. And considering the remote location, suppose so many people and their vehicles show up, the congestion on the few access roads will isolate everyone and leave them helpless to leave. He chews over this disastrous scenario before confessing his concern to Ives. But almost instantly Ives begins to laugh, and so hard that tears come to his eyes. He then pats Milhaud lightly on the shoulder as he shakes his head and assures him that he really only needs to worry that some fans show up.

Francis Poulenc is now obsessed with an entirely separate problem. Having learned that Shostakovich and Prokofiev are headed along separate musical paths, once again he recognizes his own deep urgency to benefit somehow and walk away this time with something that is more than nothing. So he confronts Hindemith determined to learn what has happened to their equipment, particularly the mixing board, microphones and mike stands, but especially the amplifiers. Hindemith turns to him and shrugs, as if ignorance and indifference are bound as inevitably as the notes of a C major chord. He assures Poulenc that whatever has happened has already happened and he shouldn't waste time struggling against something that already exists.

Poulenc becomes instantly furious although whether over the loss of equipment or over Hindemith's condescension little matters.

Bela Bartok, returned from his most recent death, asks what all this talk of some ludicrous music festival has to do with a reality anyone recognizes. Hasn't everyone been told that there is no Santa Claus or Tooth Fairy, or Easter Bunny, or Free Lunch? And anyway, even if any one of those did exist, there would still not be anything more delusional than a music festival involving modern western classical music which by itself, would have no appeal to Santa Claus, the Tooth Fairy or the Easter Bunny let alone the Hallowed Spirit of the Free Lunch (in fact, it is rumored that Santa Claus prefers country-and-western music, although this remains a rumor since he continues to resist interviews).

But now and finally Honegger feels so confident about this festival he is almost nauseously optimistic. Even as he reviews preparations and locks down logistical issues, he plans the festival's promotion; radio and television and newspapers but also posters plastered in every bar and nightclub and restaurant, particularly those where modern western classical music is performed, as well as those shops where fans purchase copies of the recorded performances of their favorite composers and their bands and their t-shirts. Honegger receives regular updates as preparation of the stage and performance area with its miles of electrical cables, towers for lighting and pyramids of amplifier cabinets relentlessly continue to grow. As these reports come in he remembers he has neither formed his own new band nor composed even a single new piece dedicated to the festival. He wonders if he is missing an opportunity to promote his own compositions of railroad locomotive music among those musicians who still find his compositions so annoying. Because after all, this is how such things work; either you work for yourself and your own benefit or you work for others and hope that works out for the best. Those fake philosophers who insist that any other form of collaboration is possible let alone desirable are silly and foolish ninnies. As his moment of triumph approaches, Honegger discovers that he wishes he had a girlfriend to enjoy all of this with, but then reflects that this may provide an unexpected chance to acquire one.

Ives remains baffled and depressed. Without much thought he discovers he hangs a lot from the disturbingly thin thread of this festival appearance where the potential for disaster is large and easily recognizable. He is so disturbed by this prospect he even contacts Wallace Stevens again to solicit his advice. But each time he calls, Stevens is either drunk or worse, and his advice is never more than burbling harangues of self-pity over why Ives believes himself better than the rest of us just because he and his dickless buddies sprinkle black dots over otherwise innocent white paper. Thus, Ives finds himself further depressed as well as annoyed.

But the day finally arrives when Honegger hears—to his nearly intoxicating relief—that preparations for this festival are complete, so that all that remains is to transport the artists and their various entourages to the performance site. The contracts for the musicians, composers, technicians and those vendors of all the necessary goods and services including security and toilets and t-shirts are signed, sealed and delivered. And so, with preparations complete and the music festival now and finally inevitable, Honegger sighs and smiles with relief; he feels no need to take even a portion of the credit, and instead is delighted simply in the knowledge that modern western classical music will be saved for one more night and so might even endure despite ignorance and hostility and oceans and mountains of silent indifference. It will endure because the music itself remains inevitable, its fixations and formulations blossoming inevitably as the fascination of so many has stamped and thereby molded modern western classical music and so deeply its appearance and evolution, being inevitable, are also therefore deathless.

And thus, despite warnings, misgivings, minor felonies and major heartbreak, this festival becomes a startling and stupendous success. To the astonishment of everyone involved, from toilet attendees to the artists, composers and performers themselves, to their managers and agents and ex-wives, the first sight of that astonishing crowd of hysterically cheering fans of every age and society all spread out over acers of the farm leaves some almost too breathless to play their instruments. Each composer and band, one after the next, is greeted with wildly frantic acclaim. Despite occasional rain and a total break-down of organization, for three days the performers and their fans celebrate the thrill and glory of modern western classical music so that even at the very end of the final day, no one involved seems prepared to go home and break up this party.

For the grand finale, Shostakovich and Prokofiev appear at either end of an empty stage grinning and waving to the crowd as they walk toward the center of the stage where finally they meet and at first crouch with their fists up, but then break into glorious grins and embrace, all to the hysterical applause of the crowd. But in the next moment the curtain behind them parts to reveal none other than Stravinsky himself and to even louder cheers he steps forward as Shostakovich and Prokofiev greet him. There the three embrace as their combined bands gather behind them and strike the opening chords of their most popular hit, "Can Anything Be Too Nice" to the hysterical delight of a crowd that seems to reach to the horizon.

With the astonishing but complete success of this festival now behind him, Honegger enjoys wave upon wave of grateful pleasure, especially since his work is now complete and he can begin his preparation to depart for greener pastures curiously littered with still-undiscovered railroad locomotives or so he has been promised. But before doing so, he begins what he already knows and recognizes even before pen touches paper must be his masterpiece, "Pacific 231".

Honegger begins his life in a small red brick house just at the edge of the railroad locomotive switching yard where his father drives the locomotives, and every night as he lays in his bed and stares at his ceiling he listens to his father drive those locomotives about with their wheezing and squealing and squeaking and clanging and groaning of metal against metal, all the while eager that one day, just like his father, he will sit up in a majestic locomotive cab looking down over that world which worships him and where he will provide for those who cannot provide for themselves. Days drift into years with Honegger hardly noticing until one day young Arthur stands beside his father in the office of the president of the railroad company. From there they all descend to the switching yard and accompany young Arthur on this his first day at his new job in command of his first railroad locomotive. Together they climb the short ladder and enter the locomotive's cab where Arthur takes his place behind the steering wheel. But suddenly and almost instantly everyone including young Arthur recognizes that he cannot see over the steering wheel while also reaching for the brake pedal.

Devastating sadness and anguish overwhelm young Arthur in the sudden but absolute recognition he will never follow in the footsteps of his father and has no future in the driving of railroad locomotives. But then, with the deepest sympathy in his voice and expression in his eyes, the president of the railroad places his hand on Honegger's shoulder and leaning slightly forward quietly suggests that with this new situation, his second-best choice of career and future is participation in that magical and mysterious world of writing compositions of modern western classical music, perhaps, besides driving a railroad locomotive, the second noblest profession on earth and where he will certainly earn very nearly as much money

And so now, with this festival settled and his role in it assured, Honegger looks about to see that with this job done and his newest masterpiece tucked beneath his arm there is nothing left for him to do; it is time and past time for him to leave. There are, after all, so many railroad locomotives whose compositions lay at the glittering foredge of his artistic future and to which he can eagerly looks forward.

Meanwhile, Charles Ives is attempting once again to play "Crystal Rowed the Boat Ashore" on his C-melody harmocarina and struggles to figure out why it sounds so weird. This remains somewhat understandable since until recently he has been dead. Besides, there are twenty-four key signatures available to composers of modern western classical music and Ives has slept with every one of them (his seminal text, "Sleeping With Key Signatures", has never gone out of print). So his difficulty does not involve a particular key signature.

Of course, all of this is taking place in Hipster Heaven.

But you've already figured that out.

A. W. DEANNUNTIS lives in Philadelphia PA. He has earned degrees from Community College of Philadelphia, Haverford College and the University of California at Davis. He has published short fiction in more than twenty periodicals. With What Books Press he has published two novels (*Master Siger's Dream* and *The Mermaid at the American Arms Motel*) and two short fiction collections (*The Final Death of Rock-and-Roll and Other Stories* and *The Mysterious Islands and Other Stories*). With Giant Claw he has published a novel (*Terror Island*) and a short fiction collection (*Magic For Martians: 49 Short Fictions*).

www.ingramcontent.com/pod-product-compliance
Lightning Source LLC
Chambersburg PA
CBHW050413110726
47899CB00008B/2691